MISS KNIGHT & THE PYRAMID'S PUZZLE

a Society for Paranormals cozy mystery

VERED EHSANI

STRAND & STONE

MISS KNIGHT & THE PYRAMID'S PUZZLE

Chapter One

I had already made up my mind to quit my position as a paranormal investigator when the summons arrived.

It was unfortunately during breakfast. I consider it the height of bad manners to give bad news at mealtime. I suspect my employer — that wily werewolf Professor Runal — knew perfectly well my feelings on the matter and sent the unwanted invitation as a provocation. Or perhaps he truly was oblivious to the requirements of relatively normal humans to eat at regular intervals.

Not that I would accuse myself of being normal. The only means by which I could approach normalcy was by ingesting medication with each meal. At the thought, I reached into my skirt pocket and stroked the small, metal pillbox. The contents of that box had allowed me to survive the past month with my sanity more or less intact, with an emphasis on 'less' rather than 'more.' But I was still here in one piece, at least physically, and able to sit with other people and converse—

"Beatrice, do stop dawdling and join us before the tea gets cold," Mrs. Steward snapped and waved me over.

"Yes, Miss Knight, join us," Lilly said, mimicking her mother's tone but adding her own particular brand of annoyance to it. My seventeen-year-old cousin was the only one to refer to me as Miss Knight, and she did so in a mocking tone.

Mrs. Steward clucked her tongue. "Really, Lilly. *Miss* Knight refers to a young, unmarried and highly eligible woman, of which your unfortunate cousin is neither. She's well past her prime."

I frowned, for I was hardly ancient. At twenty-four years of age, I should really be considered only *slightly* past the optimum marriageable age.

"But she *is* single," Lilly insisted.

"Single by virtue of being a widow is not the same as single by virtue of being virtuous and therefore of marriageable status," Mrs. Steward explained without any regard to my feelings on the matter.

I said nothing. I had long since learned that silence was usually the most suitable response to my aunt and her wayward daughter, particularly when it came to the topics of marriage and fashion. Mrs. Steward held an unhealthy obsession regarding her daughter's marital prospects, and Lilly possessed an equally unhealthy and outrageous fixation on fashion and fashionable young men.

Mr. Steward wisely said nothing at all but continued to leaf through the newspaper, doing his best to ignore both his wife and his female offspring.

I took my seat at the table, reminding myself that this was now my lot in life. Queen Victoria might rule the British Empire, but the state of women hadn't radically changed as a result.

Facts were facts. I was a widow in the year of our Lord 1898. Worse than that, I was not a wealthy widow. My employment with the Society for Paranormals provided me with a modest income, but it wasn't enough to live comfortably on my own unless I wished to live among the slum dwellers. Poverty not being particularly attractive to me, I had decided a few weeks ago to return to my aunt and uncle's home.

"Have you seen the fashion for this year's coming out season, Lilly?" Mrs. Steward asked and began pouring tea.

The change of topic suited the two women's dispositions perfectly. Lilly flicked a hand against her perfectly curled hair and giggled. "They're absolutely darling, Mama. I hope they are as exquisite when it's my turn next year."

Mr. Steward harrumphed. "Expensive is more like it," he muttered, then lifted up the newspaper to hide his face from the stern look his wife gave him.

"And what is expense when it comes to our daughter's happiness and future marriage prospects, Mr. Steward?" Mrs. Steward demanded, her voice rising into a perfectly tuned shrill that was almost sharp enough to puncture the newspaper.

"Quite right, dear," Mr. Steward hastily amended his position. "I stand corrected. The degree of fashion and the price associated with Lilly's dress will surely be in direct proportion to her opportunities for a successful marriage."

Mrs. Steward narrowed her eyes as if suspecting her husband of sarcasm or — worse still — playing with her nerves. I was pleasantly surprised she hadn't yet mentioned the delicate state of those nerves, since they seemed to feature in almost every conversation. I sipped my tea and imagined I wasn't back in my relatives' home as a dependent.

Oh, Gideon, I silently bemoaned my fate. *How your death has greatly inconvenienced me.*

"No cost is too great for the long-term benefit of our only daughter," Mrs. Steward asserted, her double chin shaking with emotion.

Only I saw Mr. Steward's hands tremble ever so slightly. The newspaper's sheets rattled against each other. It was only for a brief moment before he firmed up his grip and continued as if nothing had happened.

"There are perhaps a few unnecessary expenses we should like to avoid," he said.

Mrs. Steward clapped her cup against the saucer with enough force to chip its base. "Truly, Mr. Steward. I am all astonishment. I've never heard of such nonsense. Are we now to avoid unnecessary expenses as if we were peasants? You do play with my nerves, sir, and they were already in a pitiable state."

I hid my smile behind my cup, for there it was: the almost obligatory reference to Mrs. Steward's fragile nerves. Sadly, they weren't so delicate that they prevented her from speaking.

Ignoring her father's monetary concerns, Lilly launched into a monologue regarding fashion trends and her much-awaited coming out presentation. Mrs. Steward encouraged her, occasionally inserting a comment regarding the suitability of marriage prospects and how the perfect dress would attract the right sort of attention. Between the two of them and their obsessions, it was a marvel I could stomach breakfast.

"May I have some pocket money, Papa?" Lilly asked.

She fluttered her large, blue eyes at her father. He continued to hide behind his newspaper and did his best to discourage her attempts to wheedle out more funds from his purse.

"Papa! Can I?"

"Perhaps we could practice some restraint this season," Mr. Steward said.

"And why should we do that?" Mrs. Steward asked when Lilly's face crumpled into a pout. "The party season is upon us, Mr. Steward. Lilly can't be seen in the same dress she wore last season. Would you wish to disgrace us, sir? Make us the laughing-stock of our friends and acquaintances? I should think not."

"Indeed, perish the thought," Mr. Steward

mumbled and withdrew funds from his pocket.

"What are you wearing, Miss Knight?" Lilly asked and wrinkled her button nose in my direction.

I glanced into the contents of my tea cup and wondered what depth was required in order to drown myself. Fortunately, I was saved from having to respond when Mrs. Steward clucked her tongue.

"Do stop mocking your cousin, Lilly. You tire my nerves. What Beatrice wears is quite beside the point. As an impoverished widow ..." She paused to frown in my direction, as if both my status as a widow and my lack of independent wealth were somehow my fault. "It hardly matters what she wears as long as it doesn't discredit our family. The benefit of having Beatrice back home is she can now accompany you on outings as your chaperone."

Her tone made it clear that it might be the only benefit of my return to the home in which I was raised since my parents' untimely demise.

"How true, Aunt Steward," I said and drowned the bitter taste in my mouth with a swallow of tea. "We wouldn't want Lilly wandering the wilds of the party season unaccompanied. What would the neighbors think?"

Mr. Steward covered his chuckle with a loud

cough.

"What are you reading?" Mrs. Steward asked, even though it was more than obvious that Mr. Steward was indulging in his morning newspaper.

Without looking over the sheets, he said, "The morning mail, my dear."

"And what is happening in the news today? One must keep abreast of global events, Lilly, dear. But not too much, because men don't want a wife who knows more than they do."

"In which case, you need not worry for Lilly's sake," I whispered.

"Well, the Spanish-American war has officially been declared," Mr. Steward said and flipped a page. "China and India are experiencing the worst case of bubonic plague in recent history. Millions may die as a result. And the Anglo-Egyptian battle with the Sudanese Mahdi rages on with no end in sight."

Mrs. Steward gasped and pulled out her lavender-scented handkerchief. She patted her plump, heavily powdered cheeks. "What an uproar!"

"And let's not forget the museum thieves, my dear," Mr. Steward said with unseemly enthusiasm. "They've successfully stolen antiquities of immense value from our own museums. Scandalous, really."

"It's beyond scandalous," the good lady of the house wailed. "Plague and wars on all fronts. And now the loss of precious British artifacts. It's an affront on our history and culture. It's too much to bear."

I cleared my throat. "Actually, most of the objects stolen by the museum thieves didn't really belong to us. I believe they came from Egypt and India."

"Both of whom are under the gracious umbrella of the British Empire," Mrs. Steward snapped. "Really, Beatrice. One would almost be forgiven for believing you sympathized with both the thieves and the inhabitants of those savage lands. The British monarchy is a civilizing force and looks after the historical contents of the world. And now, some common thief robs us of everything."

I didn't bother to mention that it was a very uncommon thief who could break into a museum's secured vault and steal numerous items without leaving a trace or a clue. Mrs. Steward and her nerves were already flustered by all of this news.

She usually focused her entire attention on the section dedicated to all matters related with the upper-class socialites, particularly who was marrying whom. Discussing headline news of a national or global persuasion tested her too much, a fact her husband knew all too well.

"What is the world coming to? I can barely tolerate it. My poor, fragile nerves." She straightened and snapped her handkerchief over the table. "Mr. Steward, I don't know why you bother to read the paper if this is going to be the result."

"Of course, my dear. Being informed is entirely overrated."

"Exactly my point. Is there any news of a more local nature?"

"Mr. Henry Lindfield of Brighton crashed his automobile, rolled it into a ditch and died, thus officially becoming the first ever fatality of an automobile accident."

"Gracious, Mr. Steward," his unhappy wife huffed. "If you have nothing pleasant to share, then please say nothing at all. Such news is hardly suitable for the dining table. Let's instead focus on the weather, shall we? The weather always makes for a good mealtime conversation, Lilly."

"Very wise, my dear wife. Let's see about the weather. Ah. Here we go. An unseasonably strong storm is due by end of week and is expected to cause all manner of chaos and—"

"Mr. Steward!"

We were saved from any additional conversation about global news and the weather by a gong.

"Oh, my, how thrilling," Mrs. Steward said, her frown immediately evaporating as she straightened up and presented the smile she reserved for public engagement. "Perhaps the invitations have already begun."

Lilly smiled and clapped her hands. I poured more tea and drowned my sorrow at the prospect of being my cousin's chaperone.

The butler marched into the breakfast room, halted in front of Mr. Steward, snapped his heels together and held out a tray. "A messenger has left an invitation," he announced.

Mrs. Steward clapped a hand against the table, rattling the nearby cutlery. "Well, let's have it over here, Charles."

Charles remained standing there, so stiff a casual observer would be forgiven for mistaking him for a statue. "It is addressed to Mrs. Beatrice Knight."

We all looked at him, and I can't say who was more surprised. Mr. Steward lowered his newspaper to gawk at Charles.

"That can't be right," Lilly said.

Mrs. Steward patted her daughter's back as if

assisting her to breathe. "Now, now, dear. I'm sure it's just a mistake."

"No, m'lady," Charles intoned, still staring straight ahead as if staring down a firing squad. "It's clearly addressed to Mrs. Knight."

"That's not fair, Mama. Where are my invitations?" Lilly asked. She pushed away from the table and dashed out of the room.

"Now see what you've done," Mrs. Steward said to no one in particular. She tossed down her napkin and hurried after Lilly.

Mr. Steward snapped his newspaper in front of his face, his only defense against the family. "Well, Beatrice. Perhaps you should attend to this invitation."

Charles took that as permission to approach me and lowered the tray to my side.

I had to bite back a groan. I recognized the lazy penmanship which had scrawled my name so loosely across the surface of the envelope. Even before I opened it and read the invitation which was really a disguised summons, I knew I was in trouble.

It seemed I had an appointment with Prof. Runal at the headquarters of the Society for Paranormals. And being summoned by the Society's director was never a good turn of events.

Chapter Two

I was grateful for an excuse to escape the confines of the Steward household but soon found myself missing the warmth of the fireplace. I would be remiss to neglect any mention of the weather: cold, the air saturated with rain and a whiff of ozone. The wind conspired with the raindrops to blow dampness against my face and hands despite my umbrella.

Still, I didn't have to endure Lilly's constant rant about fashion or Mrs. Steward's insistence that Lilly could easily find a high-ranking officer at an upcoming party. But there was another issue that plagued me as I hurried along the wet streets.

Koki.

The whisper of that name caused me to shudder, and I wished I could blame the cold. I glanced over my shoulder compulsively, searching the shadows tucked inside of alleys and narrow streets. There was no sign of the shapeshifting, West African she-demon who haunted my dreams.

The last words she shouted at me — a curse and a promise — still echoed in my mind. Awake or asleep, I could picture her terrible form as she shrieked, "I swear I will find you. I will tear you limb by limb …"

I quickened my pace and arrived at the Society's building promptly at ten. The professor must have been staring out the window, for he hollered from his first-floor office above the entrance, "Come in, Beatrice, my dear. Do come in. At once!"

I lifted my chin, straightened my back and gave myself a quiet word of encouragement. This was it. This was the morning I presented my resignation. My firm and unequivocal resignation.

"And whatever he might try," I whispered as I stepped out of the rain, "however he might attempt to convince you against it, just give him the letter and be done with it."

I climbed the stairs to the first floor and silently rehearsed my speech while reminding myself of all the reasons this was a good decision. No, not just a good decision. A *great* decision. I would rather be an impoverished dependent relying on the charity of my relatives than risk another deadly encounter like the ones I'd experienced lately. In particular, the one that resulted in the death of my husband Gideon Knight.

I swallowed a sob before it rendered me incoherent and was grateful I'd taken my morning medication. Those pills were the only reason I could sleep more than a few hours without nightmares. They gave me normalcy. They prevented me from seeing ghosts or people's energy fields. They allowed me to pretend that I could possess — if not enjoy — a life approaching that of a normal human woman.

Today was the day I took one more step along that comfortably mundane path. "It's a great decision," I repeated, the words becoming a mantra.

I paused in front of a door and stared at the plaque. "Prof. Runal, Director." There was no indication of what he directed. Either a visitor knew and didn't need a reminder, or didn't know and had no business there to begin with.

I gripped the handle and was about to open the door when it was yanked open from the inside. I stumbled forward and bumped against the large girth of Prof. Runal.

Everything about the professor was big: his voice, his height, his build, the beard that covered his large jowls. Even his nose was big and quite out of proportion even for his sizable face.

"All the better to smell you with, my dear," he often joked about his substantial nose. It wasn't really a joke, coming from one of his kind.

Speaking of smells, I avoided breathing too deeply. Although his body odor was no fault of his own, the wet, doggy stench of a werewolf was one of my least favorite smells.

"There, there, Beatrice, dear," he bellowed, even though we were now standing chest to nose. "No point in falling on your face, now is there? No, indeed. We don't want you falling on anything. Well, come on in. What a day. What weather! It's a marvel humans have survived so long as a species."

With that, he ushered me in and slammed the door against the draft whistling up the staircase.

He led me through a small waiting room and into his office. The building had an empty feel to it, as one would expect on a Sunday morning. The other Society agents were either on a well-deserved weekend or undercover somewhere.

I had managed to avoid all assignments, using my recently acquired widowhood as an excuse. But now it had been a month, and I knew Prof. Runal well enough to believe he was going to assign me a new mission. Hence, the letter of resignation weighing heavy in my pocket next to the pillbox.

"A cup of tea, shall we, Beatrice? I do believe it would go down perfectly. Warm those bones, what say you?"

He didn't wait for me to say anything at all but immediately poured hot tea into an oversized cup, one that matched his stature and personality perfectly. He placed it in front of me as I sat across from him, the desk between us.

He pulled out a pendulum as was his habit whenever we met. He placed it on the desk and tapped one of the spheres with a large, stubby finger. The five bronze spheres began clicking against each other in a back-and-forth motion. *Clink ... clink ... clink ...*

He claimed the device emitted a frequency which distorted the sound of our voices for anyone lurking outside. It was a useful contraption for someone who was concerned about spies and eavesdroppers.

"Well, well, Beatrice. Well, indeed," he said and sat.

I marveled how his chair could support his weight. As it was, the spindly legs seemed to shudder, as if struggling to hold him up while resisting the force of gravity. But hold they did, and he picked up his oversized cup in sausage-sized fingers and gazed kindly through the steam.

"And how have you been, Beatrice? Tell me. Tell me everything."

I gave myself a few extra moments to consider my response and sipped at the tea. And since no inspiration was forthcoming, I continued to sip until I'd drained the cup past the halfway mark. Then I clutched it in my hands, allowing the heated porcelain to warm my thin, freezing hands. *It's a great decision*, I reminded myself.

Clink … clink … clink …

"To be honest, professor—"

"Yes, absolutely. Let's be honest, please! I always prefer honesty above all things, Beatrice. Truthfulness first and foremost, I say. So please go ahead and tell me everything." His eyes sparkled under a pair of eyebrows as thick as hairy caterpillars and just as animated.

"I was considering ..." I swallowed hard. Why was this so difficult?

"Yes?"

I cleared my throat and set my cup down on the desk. Before I lost my nerve completely, I reached into my pocket, withdrew the folded letter and slid it across the wooden surface toward him. "I believe you'll find all the details in here. But in short, I'm submitting my resignation from the Society."

The professor sagged against the backrest, the chair once again creaking and groaning in protest. I couldn't look at his astonished expression, so I glanced at the wall to one side where my eyes fell upon a piece of parchment encased in a metal frame. How well I remembered it and the words written in beautiful calligraphy.

The first time I'd ever entered this office was as a child. Prof. Runal was posing as a child therapist, for my parents were convinced there was something wrong with me and that I needed to be institutionalized at once. The dismal options were either a nunnery or an insane asylum. The professor protected me from both options.

The framed calligraphy had been on the wall back then just as it was now. I silently read it in order to calm my nerves.

Mandates of the Society for Paranormals & Curious Animals to which all its members pledge:

Investigate, document and — when appropriate — enroll into the Society new individuals and species;

Maintain the secrecy of the Paranormal Realm in general, and the Society and its activities specifically;

Ensure all members commit themselves to this mandate and to the directives of the Society's Council.

A deep cough startled me out of my reverie, and I swiveled in my chair to face the professor. As difficult as it was, I forced myself to meet his worried gaze and tried not to inhale too deeply.

Clink ... clink ... clink ... The pendulum's five spheres marked out the passing seconds.

"Well, this is a surprise, Beatrice. A shock, if I'm to be honest, which I am, as we've already discussed. Astonishing, really," he said. "In fact, I shall put it down as a residue of your grief and the trauma you've recently experienced. We shall speak no more of it. Not one word."

"But sir—"

"Not a word." He held up a hand as if it could stop the words from pouring out of me. "It's all quite understood and forgiven. Now, on to the matter at hand."

"But my resignation—"

"Ah, yes. That unfortunate incident. But remember. We shall speak no more of it. Because of course how could you resign? You are by far my star investigator, the best at finding those supernatural elements who refuse to comply with our lofty mandates. And we know we cannot have that. For what shall happen to the wider society? Chaos. Confusion. And quite possibly a disruption in the supply of tea."

We both shuddered at the horror of such an outcome.

"So you see, Beatrice, my dear. You now understand we must go forward. Resignation is simply not an option we can consider. And this is the perfect opportunity to introduce the matter in which your assistance is greatly needed. We have a mission for you."

Chapter Three

We have a mission for you.

I tried not to shudder at his words. Instead, I forced myself to meet his warm gaze, a gaze that was more fatherly than that of my own father. It was certainly more accepting, more loving, more embracing than the Stewards had ever been, despite them being my blood relatives.

As I sat before this werewolf who had quite literally saved me from a life in one institution or another, who had trained me and given me opportunities no woman in Victorian England could ever imagine, I wondered if he was right. Could I really resign, after all he had provided me?

I nodded, not sure what the answer was. "Of course, sir. Please proceed."

"Excellent! Marvelous. Now, I know how you feel about travel these days, and I do understand. After that mix-up in Lagos …" He shook his large head and sighed.

Mix-up? It was more like a massacre. Despite the understatement, my stomach squirmed. His attempt at sympathy meant I was in trouble. My lungs ceased functioning for a moment, leaving me light-headed and wishing I'd delivered my resignation through the mail.

"I'm delighted to hear that, sir," I finally managed to say in between the *clink … clink … clink* … of the pendulum's five bronze spheres.

"That's why you'll be going to Egypt instead."

"Egypt!"

"Yes, as fine a location as any."

"Sir. With all due respect, I'd rather not be traveling anywhere farther than East London."

"Nonsense! Ridiculous! Poppycock!" Prof. Runal often spoke in exclamation marks. "Where's your spirit of adventure?"

"I believe I left it in West Africa."

"But you won't be anywhere near West Africa, Beatrice. You'll be in Egypt, which is practically in the Middle East. And as everyone knows, the Middle East is Europe's backyard, so to speak."

I stood up, went to a side table and picked up the globe sitting there. The globe was bigger than my head and a lot older, its leather surface covered in minute, hand-painted details. My fingers brushed over borders and oceans until they found the continent of Africa. "Egypt is here, sir. It's almost next to Nigeria."

"Hardly. There are a few bits of real estate in between."

"Not nearly enough."

"It'll be fine. Perfectly acceptable. A breeze, particularly when compared to your last mission in that vicinity."

I traced the outline of Africa. It looked like an apostrophe connecting *it* with *is a bad idea*.

"And there's no time to lose, Beatrice. None at all."

I returned to my chair and tried not to squirm. This whole scenario reminded me of that fateful trip to Lagos. It had been more than a year ago, shortly before I met and married Gideon Knight. But the memories of those few fateful days had been forcefully imprinted in my mind as if with a red-hot brand. They still sizzled painfully, just as the memory of Gideon's last hour on this earthly plane pulsed with unhealthy intensity.

"I can't just leave," I spluttered as I scrambled for a valid reason to support my statement. "What would my aunt say? More importantly, what would the neighbors say? A young widow gallivanting around the world. It's scandalous."

The old werewolf shrugged. "Does it matter?"

"Of course it does. It matters to me, and certainly to my poor aunt, whose nerves are frayed at the best of times."

"If you say so." Prof. Runal tapped the side of his gargantuan nose. "There's nothing for it, then. We'll have to devise a story, an excuse so grand and elaborate they'll have to believe it and therefore grant you permission to go."

"I don't want to go."

"Rubbish! Of course you do. It's a fantastical adventure, it is! Now all that's left is to create a socially acceptable story. With what do young women occupy themselves these days?"

"Fashion and finding a husband."

"Splendid! Superb! Quite brilliant, really. I'm sure we can arrange a husband or lover or something to that effect. Yes, we jolly well can."

"We jolly well cannot!" I said.

His large eyes blinked several times, and he leaned away from me. "I see."

Clink … clink…

"Surely ladies travel these days," Prof. Runal said, his tone cautious.

"To visit nearby family, perhaps."

He smiled, his large teeth gleaming. "Then we shall say you're visiting family. There's nothing easier than family."

"I have no family apart from the Stewards, and they are anything but easy."

"There's no need to involve them, Beatrice. I'm certain we can rummage around and find some distant relatives or some such thing."

"None I'd want to visit."

"This is unnecessarily difficult." He rubbed his forehead as if trying to erase the deep frown. "What if we sent you with a chaperone on an educational voyage? Young ladies on occasion do seek to improve their minds, do they not?"

"Who would be my chaperone?"

"Why, me, of course! It's marvelous, magnificent—"

"It's unacceptable, sir."

"Quite right, my dear. I'm far too busy for traipsing about the world, pretending to be your chaperone. But sacrifices must be made, my dear. Sacrifices! So it is decided. I shall pose as your chaperone. An uncle, perhaps. Yes, I think that might work. And you should probably be an unwed niece."

"And when are you suggesting we leave?"

"Immediately. Right now. As soon as humanly and inhumanly possible."

"Which would be …" I left the sentence hanging.

"There is a steamship leaving this very evening. Tonight. We shall dine with the captain, in fact."

"Tonight? You want us to go tonight?"

"I want us to go immediately. This morning, if possible. But alas, ships to Cairo are not so frequent. So we shall go this evening."

"But surely this mission can wait a day or a week?" I'd intended to sound confident and commanding, but my voice warbled at the end.

"Absolutely not, Beatrice. Not at all. Out of the question." He leaned closer to me and glanced at the pendulum ticking back and forth. The metal balls continued to click pleasantly against each other, the soft *clink* filling in the spaces between our words. "You see, I've been followed lately."

I thought of Koki, of her promise and threat. I lowered my hands onto my lap before the professor could see how they shook. "By whom?"

"By agents opposed to the pursuits of the Society! Nefarious beings who are against the Empire and our queen, who would undermine and even destroy our efforts to protect those paranormals who agree to abide by the Society's mandates. They are after me. Or more specifically, after this artifact."

The scraping of a drawer opening filled the silence between us. He reached in and brought out a small bag. It looked like a velvet sachet used by some women to hold their jewelry.

Prof. Runal opened the drawstring, his fingers dexterous despite their size, and removed a paperweight in the shape of a prism. From what I'd seen of photos and paintings, it was a perfect replica of one of the Egyptian pyramids. Its base was not much bigger than the palm of my hand.

"All this fuss for that?" I asked.

"Indeed, it might not seem particularly impressive, Beatrice, nothing to look at," Prof. Runal said and tapped the tip of the pyramid. "But looks can be deceiving, as well we know. Don't we, Beatrice? Misleading, indeed. For this little replica is the key to ending the war which the British Empire and its allies are waging against the Sudanese rebels."

I couldn't stop the frown that wrinkled my forehead. Mrs. Steward was fond of reminding us that no man wanted a wrinkled woman, particularly when those wrinkles were created by frowning. "Keep your expression smooth and unsullied by emotion, girls," she'd lecture us.

Then again, I was now well past my prime in terms of getting married. So I chose to ignore her sage advice regarding the preservation of smooth skin and frowned at the small pyramid. "I can't see how that provides the key to anything but a child's amusement."

"Indeed. Some mysteries are hard to fathom. But I have it on good authority that this is a critical component to providing the Egyptians the motivation and inspiration they need to help us end this war. And so we must travel to Cairo and return it to its rightful owner."

"Surely this can be delivered through the mail or by a courier?"

"Surely not. Have you not been listening at all, Beatrice? Please do pay attention. I've been followed, my dear. Shadowed and stalked! Do you think those agents of chaos wouldn't follow the mail or a courier and intercept it on the way? No, Beatrice. The only solution, the only means by which we can ensure this object is placed in the correct hands, is if we ourselves take it directly. Between the two of us, we shall be a formidable force against any who dare try to steal it."

"I see," I said, even though I wasn't entirely convinced. "But there are other Society investigators who would be a better fit for this task."

"Their fitness is debatable. Besides, what better deception than for a young woman innocent of the appearance of strength and cunning to carry it? In fact, I suggest we introduce you as Miss Knight, to encourage this false perception."

"Sir, that's hardly appropriate—"

"No one need be the wiser, my dear."

My hand strayed into my jacket pocket and stroked the small metal pillbox. "And do you anticipate any need for me to study energy fields and the like?"

"Oh, I doubt it will come to that, Beatrice. Highly improbable. For I intend to confuse the agents that currently follow me and encourage them to believe I've gone to Dublin. The trip to Cairo will be closer to a holiday cruise rather than a mission. You deserve a vacation, my dear, after all that has transpired recently."

In the pause, he studied me, his eyes glowing with compassion.

I gripped the pillbox — my tether to normalcy — and tried to smile. "Well, at the very least, it will give me a break from this incessant rain and damp cold," I said with forced enthusiasm, thus capitulating to his request.

Prof. Runal beamed, his wide smile brightening his face. "That's the spirit, Beatrice. That's the attitude that makes you such a fine investigator and so perfect for this mission. Yes, we shall escape the late winter rains and enjoy a bit of sunshine. You'll see, Beatrice, my dear. It shall be as easy as a cruise in the sunshine. As easy as that and just as relaxing."

And although I couldn't possibly anticipate at that point how wrong he truly was, I suspected even then it wouldn't be so easy after all.

Chapter Four

As I didn't have many outfits from which to choose, it didn't take me long to pack what I needed. In short order, I'd made some excuse to the Steward family about visiting a dying friend in the countryside, packed my valise with a few outfits and left for the port.

Prof. Runal was waiting for me at the base of the gangplank. I joined him and stared at the vessel before me. An uncharacteristically violent spell of nervous energy gripped me to the point that I couldn't take another step.

The steamship, the S.S. *Suez*, reminded me of the ship that had carried me to Lagos. The similarities were not reassuring.

"Come now, my dear, let us proceed," Prof.

Runal said. "Remember, this is a holiday, really." He was standing immediately behind me, his physical bulk looming over me.

Sadly, that wasn't the only thing looming over me. In a fit of mischievousness, the wind whirled around us and enveloped me in a swirl of werewolf stench. And while I could never blame Prof. Runal for his lack of hygiene, the odor propelled me up the gangplank faster than his reassurances that this would be an easy trip.

Once I stepped onto the deck, I inhaled deeply. The sailors were scurrying around, preparing the ship, loading the supplies and generally ignoring the passengers. And while they were not bathing as frequently as I would wish them to, at least they didn't smell like a werewolf.

"Junior Second Officer Mallory, at your service," a young man with deeply tanned skin announced as he stepped in front of me and saluted.

I glanced between him and the professor, unsure if I was expected to salute him back.

"Jolly good, Junior Officer … that is, Second Junior … Mallory," Prof. Runal said in his booming voice that reached the other side of the deck and startled a sailor who was barely old enough to shave. "You may show us to our quarters, if you would, sir."

Junior Second Officer Mallory clicked his heels, which reminded me of our butler. He spun around and marched across the deck to a door that led down a steep set of stairs. He proceeded to lead us through corridors that were oppressively narrow and dark.

I was tempted to inform the junior officer that I preferred to sleep on deck. Somehow, I knew he would protest. And if he didn't, the senior second officer probably would.

"For the gentleman," Mallory said and gestured to a room that was hardly bigger than a water closet.

Prof. Runal sniffed, his nostrils flaring as if inspecting the smells left by the previous tenant. "And this is first class?"

"Indeed, sir. Our very best."

"Then I shudder to see your very worst, young man, indeed I do," the professor said before squeezing himself through the slim entrance and into his quarters.

It was fortunate we had both packed lightly, but even the rucksack slung over Prof. Runal's shoulder bumped against the bed and the door at the same time.

"My, my," Prof. Runal murmured as he tried to angle his bag until he could slide it under the low ledge that served as a bed. "I think I shall be spending much time on the deck. As much as possible, in fact. Would you care to join me for a promenade before dinner, Beatrice?"

Young Mallory's eyebrows rose at the professor's casual use of my first name. Prof. Runal was oblivious to such social niceties. We might have to use the story that I was his niece, at the very least.

"I shall join you shortly, sir," I said and allowed Mallory to lead me deeper into the bowels of the ship. Not that we were going to a lower level, but the longer we walked, the more distant the doorway to sun, air and rain felt.

"And the quarters for the young lady," Mallory said and partially bowed, not looking at me.

"Thank you."

He nodded stiffly and strode back the way we'd come.

The room was barely bigger than the narrow bed, with only a round window facing the outside, a tiny excuse of a closet and a small chair.

I used my sleeve to wipe a smear off of the window and peered at the view. The day was rapidly wasting away into darkness, and the rain had not let up. A more dismal evening I couldn't imagine. And while it was claustrophobic in here, I wondered how long I could bear to be above deck in such inclement weather.

I quickly unpacked what little I had brought. Thus settled, I picked up the one item without which I never left home: an oxide green metal walking stick. Some might think me infirm when they see me strolling about with it in hand. Others have remarked that it's an unfashionable accessory with its bronze fist perched on top.

The truth was I wasn't an invalid, nor was the walking stick a fashion piece. It was in fact a most useful piece of equipment, gifted to me by the professor once I'd graduated from my basic training course. Various knobs and levers caused an assortment of tools to become accessible. From the bottom, a wickedly sharp blade will emerge. Another slot will reveal a blowgun with several darts already anointed with sleeping potion. It was a most formidable weapon precisely because it didn't look like one.

With it in my grip, I began to feel more reassured that perhaps the professor was correct. I became even more confident once the anchor was raised, and the ship pulled away from the dock without any disturbing event occurring. I was so buoyed by the utter lack of excitement that I joined the professor for a quick stroll around deck before dinner.

Once land was a fading memory, we were summoned for dinner by a cheerful bell. The first-class dining room was as elegant a space as any I could find in the high streets of London. Appointed with kerosene lanterns, dark wood paneling and rich tapestries, the place had a cheerful, warm glow that quickly dispelled the dampness of outside.

An older man on spindly, bowed legs rushed toward us as we entered the diner. His face was deeply creased by exposure to the elements, and a permanent frown etched into his brow.

"Prof. Runal and guest?" he asked and waited for one of us to acknowledge the fact. "I'm Chief Steward Franklin Stewart."

"Goodness, that's a mouthful," I said under my breath.

Prof. Runal smiled, having of course heard me.

Chief Steward Stewart had not and continued talking, hardly pausing for breath. "Captain James McCormick has requested your presence at his table." His frown deepened. He paused, as if waiting for us to respond. When we remained silent and expectant, he added, "It's quite an honor. He doesn't always have time to join the guests for meals. Follow me."

With that, he did a sharp turn and hurried between the tables to the head table.

Prof. Runal leaned toward me and winked. "You see, Beatrice. First class all the way. Consider this a well-deserved holiday."

"With all due respect, sir, I can think of more appropriate locations for a holiday."

He bellowed a laugh that shook his body and a nearby waiter. "You are as usual amusing, Beatrice. For what finer holiday can there be but on an isolated ship in the middle of the stormy seas? Indeed, there is none."

While I was tempted to laugh at his joke, I didn't because he wasn't joking. This was exactly the sort of situation the old werewolf enjoyed. A moment later, we were seated at Captain McCormick's table.

As I sat, something brushed up against my ankle. I gasped and jumped away from my chair just as something with yellow eyes crept toward me and hissed.

Chapter Five

Walking stick held before me in case the creature attacked, I asked, "What is that … that *thing* doing here?"

"My apologies, miss," the captain said and rubbed his bushy beard as if unsure what else to do. "It's the cat, you see. Come here, girl, and stop bothering the guests."

He snapped his fingers, and a black cat slunk toward him and wrapped itself around his legs, purring loudly. It stared at me until the captain picked the beast up and held it as if it were a treasured baby.

"I was not aware pets were permitted on board," I said as the chief steward assisted me to push in my chair.

Captain McCormick smiled. "Not a pet, Miss ..." He waited for me to fill in the appropriate name.

I hesitated, as I couldn't very well call myself Mrs. Knight. That would raise far too many questions, the first being how I was traveling on such a wild excursion without my husband, but instead in the company of an older man who looked like he was related to a wild dog rather than a young woman. The alternative was slightly less scandalous, so I decided to follow Prof. Runal's advice.

"Miss Knight. I'm traveling with my uncle." I gestured to the professor and hoped he wouldn't say otherwise.

"Indeed, my dear niece is quite the adventurous type," Prof. Runal said and chuckled. "Quite intrepid, if I might say."

Captain McCormick glanced between the two of us, as if unsure what my level of adventurousness had to do with anything. "We always keep a cat on board, Miss Knight. Ports are infamous for rats, and the cats do very well to keep the ship clear of them. Sadly, my old one died just as we were preparing for this voyage, and I hate to travel without a cat. I found this one wandering the dock. She's quite a pretty creature, isn't she?" He rubbed the cat behind its perky ears, and the creature rewarded him with a loud, deep purr.

"Delightful," I said, wishing they would hurry up and present us with food rather than cats. I'd never been one of those women who pretended not to require much sustenance. In fact, I became rather cranky unless fed on a regular basis, and I was fast approaching the limit of my endurance.

"Her name's Cairo," the captain continued, oblivious to my rumbling stomach. "Since the ship most frequently goes to that city, I felt Cairo would be a good name for it. Don't you agree, Miss Knight?"

"If you say so, sir. Will we be starting dinner soon?"

It seemed my suggestion that I had an appetite which required attention startled the dear captain, for he gawked at me before setting the cat down. "Chief Steward Stewart, if you will."

"Well, it really is about time," I said softly enough that only Prof. Runal could hear me.

He chuckled appreciatively. "Indeed, a bit of food will go a long way. Otherwise, I might be tempted to eat that cat. It did look rather plump, didn't it?"

I cleared my throat in agreement. The captain

had no idea what sort of appetite a werewolf could have, and I prayed the chief steward had sufficiently stocked the reserves for the two-week trip, for between Prof. Runal and myself, we would need to be well-fed.

The captain then introduced us to the other senior crew members who had joined his table for the evening: Chief Engineer Richard McIntyre and Chief Officer Pierre Montaigne.

"There's a lot of chiefs and officers around here," I whispered to Prof. Runal. "I hope we're not expected to remember all of them."

"Only if they commit a crime, my dear."

The chief engineer downed his wine like it was water, then leaned toward us and winked. "Oi, Pierre! Pass us a spot of wine, will ya, lad?" he shouted in a Scottish accent thick enough to cut with a butter knife. "And maybe the wee lassie would like some, as well. Come on, then. Don't keep us waiting, Frenchy, me mate."

The captain hid a smile while Chief Officer Frenchy bestowed a haughty glare at his fellow crew member. "Monsieur engineer," he said, his French accent no less pronounced, "Zis informalité is not ze way."

The chief engineer laughed. "Stop being so formal, you old frog."

"That's enough, Rocky," the captain warned, then turned to me. "As you can see, we have quite a diverse crew."

I refrained from commenting that it was far from diverse, there being neither a woman nor a paranormal working under his flag. Then again, in the world as it was, we were unlikely to see a female sailor.

I glanced around at our fellow first-class passengers. There were all total close to thirty of us, seated at tables of two, four or six. One stylishly dressed woman caught my gaze. She wore a red feather boa and a black felt hat topped with a cluster of black feathers — both accessories being currently in vogue, according to what I'd overheard from Lilly.

The fashionable woman narrowed her eyes at me, as if somehow I had gravely insulted her by studying her attire. She shifted her chair in order to turn her back to me. Her companion — a man with a top hat, a narrow mustache and a knowing smirk — studied me in return before his female companion snapped her fingers to recapture his attention.

"You've taken an interest in our most prominent

guests, Miss Knight," the captain said and nodded with approval. "Lord Voleur and his sister Lady Larrona often grace our ship. They frequently holiday in Cairo."

I swallowed my disbelieving snort with a mouthful of salad. They were as likely to be siblings as Prof. Runal was my uncle, but their business was their own.

"Beatrice, my dear," the professor whispered and leaned toward me. His whisper was not a small thing, but with the general background chatter, clink of cutlery and serving staff rushing back and forth with platters full of dishes, his words went unheard by any except myself. "I have one favor I must ask of you."

"Beyond requesting my presence on this trip?"

"As you say. But this is a far graver and perhaps more important one. Remember the object I showed you in my office?"

For a moment, I thought he was referring to the pendulum. But something about the crook of his hairy eyebrows made me reflect more deeply. "You mean that—"

"Not a word," he warned. "I must ask if you can keep the item with you at all times. As a young, innocent-looking woman, you are above suspicion."

"Hardly. People saw us arrive together. I'm sitting next to you. Surely I've become guilty by association."

He chuckled. "Perhaps, but not likely. On the off chance the agents in question followed me on board, it is best you tuck the item away. Women are always carrying around purses and sachets and similar unnecessary accessories, are they not? It won't seem at all odd for you to keep a purse on your shoulder. On the other hand, it might be rather peculiar if I were to carry one. It's not something men do."

"Then perhaps people should rethink men's fashion. For as we've now seen, a purse is in fact quite a practical accessory."

"Indeed, Beatrice. You are quite correct. But as we are not in charge of fashion, might I ask you to take this burden upon yourself?"

At that moment, Chief Steward Stewart slid a bowl of pea soup before me. The flavors floated up in the steam, tickling my nose, tantalizing my olfactory nerves which in turn caused me to salivate in anticipation. "Of course."

"Excellent. I'm so glad you agree, for I took the liberty of slipping it into your purse upon our arrival in the dining room."

I glanced at him, opened my mouth to protest at his presumption, then plunged my spoon into the soup instead. After all, the deed was done, and my stomach had had quite enough of conversation for the night.

"And one last point."

I paused, the spoon almost touching my lips. "Yes?"

"Do keep an eye out, will you? And by that, you know what I mean."

I thrust the spoon in my mouth, scalding my tongue. Yes, I did indeed know. My other hand slipped into my jacket pocket and clenched the pillbox.

"Beatrice?"

I swallowed hard, a trail of soup scorching my throat. "Of course, sir."

After all, what harm could possibly happen if I skipped the medicine for one night?

Chapter Six

I blamed what happened next on the second helping of chocolate pudding.

What was Chief Steward Stewart thinking by ordering an excess of pudding and displaying it so alluringly? And on our first night! I can resist many a temptation, but chocolate pudding doesn't make that list. As a result of the chief steward's thoughtlessness, I had two generous helpings.

Later that night, I tossed and turned for a while on my narrow bunk, silently cursing the delicious pudding which now broiled and bubbled in my stomach. I almost took one of my pills, Prof. Runal's request be damned. I fell asleep before I could, and a six-legged monstrosity entered my dreams.

I was back in Lagos, running through the constabulary. The sights, sounds and smells of death bombarded me from all sides. But I was still alive by some miracle and determined to keep it that way.

I raced up the open stairway, the only path left to me, and dashed into the first room I found with an open door. And while I didn't think the lock could possibly work against the shapeshifting demon stalking me, I bolted the door and hid in a closet.

The thud of an elephant-sized praying mantis approached the door. The sharp tips of its legs scratched against wood and rock. And then the door exploded in a shower of wooden splinters. The creature ripped open the door to the closet and dragged me out. It towered over me, its large pincers snapping below its triangular head.

"I told you I would find you, little girl," Koki said, her pincers approaching my neck. "There is nowhere you can hide. There's no place far enough or safe—"

Before she could decapitate me, the ground opened up, and I fell down a long tunnel.

I landed in a familiar room. I was back home in

the apartment I shared for a precious year with my husband. Gideon Knight was there, a frown marring his handsome features. He was arguing with someone, defending me, and I knew that was a bad idea. Noble but dangerous.

"Gideon?"

He didn't listen to me. Instead, he stood up, hands curling into tight fists as he prepared to protect me from …

From whom?

The dreamworld was blurry, and for a moment, I thought it was the mantis. She'd somehow tracked me down in London, just like she'd promised she would do. But no, the mantis wasn't the threat.

I started to scream, desperate to warn Gideon. But the air between us was thick, muffling my voice, holding me back. No matter how much I screamed and pushed forward, I didn't move, and my words shattered against an invisible wall.

And right before he died, Gideon turned his beautiful eyes toward me. "This is on you, Beatrice. Now wake up."

I pounded my fists against the invisible wall, but it was too late. The home I shared with Gideon dissolved around me until there was only darkness.

"Wake up, Beatrice."

I jerked awake, flailing my arms at the darkness which crowded in on me. The sounds of waves brushed against my ears, and for a second, I thought I'd fallen into the dark pond outside my childhood home.

"You're on the steamer," I whispered. "It was just a dream. A really bad, vivid dream. That blasted pudding. I shall have words with the steward."

"Wake up, Beatrice!"

The whispered echo of Gideon's voice removed the last vestige of sleepiness. I sat up in time to see a shadow darker than the other shadows slip silently into the room. My door was ajar, even though I'd locked it before going to bed.

I've never been one for screaming and other stereotypically feminine theatrics. But I must admit there were times when a well-placed, high-pitched scream did produce marvelous results. I decided this was one such occasion. I reached for my walking stick, held it up like a bat just in case the intruder approached me, and began to scream like someone was trying to kill me.

The shadow startled and stepped toward me with an inhuman stealth and grace. I continued to scream while kicking my legs free of the blankets. Already, my wordless plea for assistance was having the desired results. A door banged opened somewhere down the hallway, and a male voice shouted while heavy feet pounded toward my cabin.

The intruder disappeared as quickly and quietly as it had arrived.

I fumbled for the matchbox on the small side table. My hand didn't shake as I lit a match and set it to the candlewick. After a moment of spluttering, a warm glow crept across my room, devouring darkness and replacing it with golden light. My door creaked all the way open, and I prepared myself to do battle.

Chief Officer Frenchy stood in the opening, holding up a kerosene lantern. The whiff of it assaulted my olfactory senses and removed any lingering doubt that this might be a dream, but I forgave him for the intrusion.

"Miss, what is ze matter?"

"Intruder. It … he … went down the other way," I shouted and gestured with my walking stick.

Frenchy took a couple steps back, eyeing my stick and making no movement to chase my intruder. "I see. A nightmare, zen? Ze seas sometimes have zat effect on ze senses. It will pass once you become accustomed to ze rolling of ze waves."

Of course the man would assume I was susceptible to such frailties as delicate nerves imposed! I huffed in frustration but didn't pursue the matter. Besides, the intruder was well gone by now.

"Beatrice? Beatrice, my dear … niece!" Prof. Runal boomed from close by. He appeared at my doorway with remarkable speed, almost pushing Frenchy into the doorjamb in his haste. "Are you quite all right, my dear?"

Frenchy shuffled out of sight and muttered, "Women. Zey shouldn't be allowed on ze ships."

I was tempted to introduce the man's thick head to my equally thick walking stick but decided against it. "I'm quite all right, *uncle*. According to our new friend, I imagined an intruder."

Prof. Runal's nostrils flared as he sniffed the room. "I believe our friend is incorrect, although I can't place the scent. Is it safe? Do you have it still?"

I reached a hand under my pillow and patted the lump resting in the corner. "Quite safe, sir."

Meanwhile, Chief Officer Frenchy was reassuring the few guests who had awoken that nothing untoward had happened, and that the young lady was quite alright and in no need of assistance apart

from a cup of chamomile tea. The second statement was now quite correct, even if the first
was not.

Prof. Runal checked the latch. "The lock is
unbroken, which means your intruder had a key."

I shuddered. "I'll bar the door better next
time."

He nodded and started to bid me good night
when we were joined by Chief Engineer Rocky
McIntyre.

"I heard you scream, lass. What's all the fuss,
now?" he asked and peered into the room.

I frowned as I no longer had any need of male
assistance. "What is the chief engineer doing
roaming about the hallways at this time of night?"

"'Tis morning, lass, though early, I grant you.
I'm a wee bit of an insomniac, myself."

"That makes one of us. Someone just tried to
forcibly enter my cabin."

The chief engineer's face settled into a craggy
scowl. "Blast them all, the wee goblins are at work
again."

"Unlikely," I said. "Goblins dislike water
intensely."

"Not these ones, lass."

I discreetly sniffed the air for traces of alcohol

or some other mind-altering substance. There was none, but I'd heard enough about sailors and their various superstitions to doubt very much that the ship was plagued by a gaggle of goblins.

Another sailor jogged into view. "Rocky, you're needed in the engine room. Something's amiss with the boiler."

"Not again," Rocky grumbled and stalked away. "I've been telling the captain for some time we need to replace Boiler A."

The sailor pressed himself against the wall to allow Rocky to pass. "No, it's Boiler C this time."

"A pox on them all."

I stared after the engineer. The sailor caught my amazed look and chuckled. "Don't mind Rocky. Heart of gold, that one."

"A golden heart is hardly useful," I instructed the ignorant sailor. "It doesn't beat, it sinks in water, and is hardly suitable in a human being who wishes to live more than a minute."

The man was clever enough to hurry after Rocky rather than stay and argue.

Prof. Runal chuckled. "Try to get some sleep, Beatrice. We shall need all our energy tomorrow."

I closed the door behind him and propped the chair under the door handle. It wasn't much, but at least it would give me notice if the intruder returned.

It took me a while to fall asleep, and just before I did, I swore I heard Gideon's voice whispering a lullaby.

Chapter Seven

"Beatrice."

"Go away," I mumbled into my pillow. "It's far too soon for another crisis, not to mention too early. Emergencies are hereby banned before breakfast."

The whispering voice persisted. "Wake up, my darling."

"No, I won't. I—"

My darling?

I jerked my face out of the pillow and rolled around, walking stick in hand. I held it over my shoulder like a spear and pressed two of the finger-nails on the bronze fist. From the other end, a wicked blade slid out.

"Whoever is in here, show yourself instantly or prepare to be impaled."

I paused and blinked sleep out of my eyes. There was no response from my uninvited visitor.

"Don't think I won't, although I'd rather not. The mess would be ghastly."

I glanced around the cabin. There wasn't much to see. Given that it was barely big enough for my bed, my valise and a chair, there was really no place for a person to hide.

Yawning, I was tempted to declare the voice a vestige of a dream and return to bed. The light sifting through the round window was watery, gray and hardly inspiring. I felt thoroughly fatigued and discouraged and could only hope more sunshine would find us as we traveled south.

But weather aside, I still had the matter of an apparently invisible intruder who was determined to wake me up. Or I was daydreaming, in which case—

"Beatrice, I'm here."

"It's bad enough my sleep was rudely interrupted by a thief last night," I said as I pressed my back to the wall and swiveled my walking stick back and forth. "But it's another matter entirely when I'm expected to converse before I've had my first pot of morning tea. Whoever you are, your manners are atrocious. And I truly cannot abide by such an absence of basic social convention."

"You're quite correct, my darling Beatrice. But can you blame me?"

The hair on the back of my neck began to prickle, which was never a good sign. The voice sounded so familiar, impossibly so. And it was becoming abundantly clear to my sleep-deprived brain that I wasn't dreaming, and that whoever was here wasn't a full-bodied person. In fact, I began to suspect I was in the presence of a non-human. A paranormal element, in other words.

Blast and double blast. So much for the professor's promise of a holiday in the sun.

I pursued the only course available to me. I squinted my eyes — how fortunate I'd neglected my medicine last night — and another layer of reality sprang into view.

I don't normally squint. For a start, it does terrible things for the skin around my eyes. And while I'm not quite as obsessed with wrinkle-free facial features as my dear Aunt Steward, she does have a point regarding the pleasantness of a woman's features being an important quality to protect. No man comes rushing to the aid of a screaming hag.

But the second and perhaps more important reason was that it was rude. I preferred to assume that an individual was a normal human until he or she proved themselves otherwise, or unless my job required me to inspect a person's true reality more closely.

However, I was facing the strangest of circumstances. An invisible person dared wake me without presenting me with a pot of tea in the process. I therefore felt it appropriate to practice a discrete amount of rudeness.

Energy sparkled around me. I continue to squint while I fumbled with one of the drawers in my walking stick. It finally slid out, revealing a small set of specially designed spectacles. They enhanced my second sight, allowing me to probe even more deeply into the hidden reality behind physical appearance.

But in this case, the spectacles were quite unnecessary. For as I squinted and began to see the currents of energy that weaved and wrapped around physical reality, a familiar outline began to form at the end of my bed. It was that of a man, and one I suspected I knew quite intimately.

My eyes popped wide open, and I gawked as the form continued to crystallize. I didn't need to squint to finally identify the person who had awoken me not only this morning, but during the night.

"Gideon?" I gasped.

There was now no mistaking it. Standing in my small cabin and far too close for comfort's sake was the ghost of my deceased and possibly murdered husband.

He was just as I remembered him. Dark brown hair waved across his forehead. Light brown eyes the color of a perfect cup of afternoon tea twinkled with merriment and mischief. I believed I might have married that man for the sake of his eyes, which I now understood was not the soundest basis for a marriage. But what did I know when I was so young and naïve?

The rest of his form filled out. He was of average height and slim build. But that charm. Oh, the charm! It was very much in evidence as he bowed from the waist, his gaze fixed on me, and a cheeky smile gracing his handsome features.

I screamed and tossed the walking stick at his head, blade first. It sailed through his body and impaled itself on the far wall. The stick reverberated loudly from the impact.

Gideon straightened, glanced over his shoulder, then back at me, his smile morphing into amazement mixed with amusement. "An excellent aim, my darling. Then again, I would expect nothing less from Mrs. Beatrice Knight, paranormal investigator extraordinaire and my wife."

"You're supposed to be dead!"

"Truly, your manners are atrocious," he said, mocking me with my own words. "I realize you haven't had your usual reviving liquids yet, but accusing one of being dead must be the height of ill manners." His smile returned, spreading across his face as he winked, then laughed. "Despite your efforts to kill me, it's still wonderful to see you. And I know you feel the same, or you will, once you recover from your shock."

I slid off the bed and strode across the cabin to my walking stick. I tugged and pulled until I could extract it from the wall. "I do believe that chocolate pudding is still working its evil magic on me, and this is nothing more than another nightmare from which I will awaken at any moment to the tantalizing scent of tea and breakfast. Until then, you should make yourself scarce."

I started to march back to the bed, determined to finish this ridiculous dream after which I planned to wake up and return to reality. And pudding was definitely off the menu for the remainder of the trip.

Instead, Gideon stepped in front of me, his face uncharacteristically serious. "Beatrice. It really is me. Who do you think woke you up when that nasty trespasser tried to break in here? I only wish I'd seen the rascal's face. We could've arrested the villain and tossed him overboard before anyone was the wiser."

I stared at him, squinting in my effort to discern the truth. And then it hit me.

I slapped one hand over my mouth to contain the shriek that was bubbling inside of me. My knees started to wobble, which was never a good sign. I put it down to low blood sugar. "Gideon? It's truly you?"

He reached out a ghostly hand and brushed it across my cheek. It felt like I was being caressed by a cool breeze. "Of course. Didn't you hear me sing that lullaby you like, the one I always sang when you had a nightmare?"

"That was … that …"

"Perhaps you should take a seat, Beatrice. We can't have you fainting. That's not what you do."

A small squeak snuck through my fingers, and I

collapsed onto the edge of the narrow bed. "Why? How? Never mind the how. Why?"

Gideon shrugged and started to fade at the edges. "Death really doesn't become me, Beatrice. Not to mention it's rather boring."

"Boring?"

"Yes. Especially as there's no one interesting with whom to converse."

"Where have you been for the past month?"

"I've been trying to get your attention, Mrs. Knight," Gideon said. "It's not like you to be so oblivious to your surroundings. I made all sorts of noise, floated in front of you, shouted in your ear. But you gave me absolutely no response. Whatever is the matter?"

I glanced at my jacket hanging over the end of my bed. The pocket with the pillbox bulged slightly. "Nothing."

Gideon scoffed. "My dear, when a woman says *nothing* in response to a man's question, it most certainly isn't *nothing*. In fact, it's quite likely the man is about to have some serious trouble on his hands, and will remain oblivious to the fact until it's far too late."

"Well, in this case, it really is nothing."

"You know I don't believe you."

"You know you're dead."

"And there it is. You're still upset about that."

"Of course I'm upset, Gideon! You're … not alive."

"How charming. I think I shall take a nap now."

"Wait, Gideon."

"I'm feeling rather tired, you know," he said, and yawned. "Must be all that excitement from last night." And with that, he faded out completely, leaving me even more alone than I was before.

Chapter Eight

The breakfast bell pulled me out of my shock at seeing the ghost of my deceased husband loitering in my room.

I quickly prepared myself to venture into public spaces, both hoping and dreading I'd see Gideon again. I was still in a daze when I entered the first-class dining room. It was not as full as it was last night, but the woman with the red feather boa and black hat was sitting at the corner table opposite the man with the narrow mustache. They both paused in their conversation to watch me enter, and didn't resume until I was seated on the far side of the room across the table from Prof. Runal.

"Are you quite well, Beatrice? How are you feeling?" he asked, his large, heavy features set in the epitome of fatherly concern.

I blinked as if coming out of a trance. "As well as can be expected, I suppose." I glanced sideways and watched the strange couple continue their whispered conversation, their heads almost touching as they leaned across their small table.

"Jolly good. Excellent! I'm glad to hear it," Prof. Runal said as he poured me a cup of tea. "Because we need to take action now."

"There's no need to discuss action until we've had breakfast, sir," I said and drained the cup of tea so fast, my tongue tingled from the scalding liquid.

I met the professor's astonished gaze. He was still holding the pot. Wordlessly, I held up my cup. Equally silent, the professor poured me a second cup which I imbibed at a slower, more measured rate.

"Are you sure—" the professor began.

"Quite. I'll be perfectly fine after a hearty breakfast."

The professor harrumphed but remained silent until I had eaten. The entire time, I studied the room as more passengers sat at their preassigned tables.

Prof. Runal leaned closer to me. "Are you thinking what I'm thinking?"

"That we need another plate of toast and a pot of tea? Absolutely."

His eyebrows lifted up. The first time I met him, those eyebrows had reminded me of plump, hairy caterpillars. They seemed to have a life of their own. Even now, the similarity often made me smile.

"I was not referring to the food, Beatrice, although I do appreciate the requirement. I mean suspects. Suspects, my dear! For as certain as sunrise, the thief will strike again."

"So much for a holiday."

"I believe our holiday cruise is finished for now. It seems I was not as careful as I had thought in making my escape yesterday. They must have sent an agent to follow us on board. Indeed, that must be what happened. And somehow, they surmised my plot to give you the item in safekeeping."

Motion from the ceiling caused me to glance upward, but there was nothing there.

"Beatrice, I need you to assist me in ascertaining who our possible suspects are," he continued, seemingly oblivious to my distracted state.

"Yes, sir," I said automatically without really

thinking deeply about his comment. Was Gideon in the ceiling, watching me?

"Excellent. Brilliant! I knew you'd agree. So we've decided, then?"

I shook my head and met his gaze. "Decided what, sir?"

"To study each and every passenger, of course. And from that research, make a list of suspects, then investigate each one of the suspects with even greater care and deeper detail. We shall continue in such a manner until we find the culprit, Beatrice!"

I gulped. "Each and every passenger?"

"The crew as well." Prof. Runal nodded, his shaggy mane flopping around his shoulders. "Indeed, the crew are as suspect as anyone else. One never knows on these ships who has been hired from what background."

I did a quick calculation based on the number of chairs. "There must be around thirty first class passengers—"

"It's exactly thirty, I believe," the professor interrupted.

"And the crew—"

"Upwards of twenty."

"And then the passengers in steerage."

He waved a hand dismissively. "Take no heed of

them. It's hardly likely that one of them snuck through the ship from the lower levels and entered first class, particularly at night. The crew locks the door between steerage and other levels shortly after dinner and only opens it again before breakfast."

I stared into my tea skeptically, as if searching for answers there. "Still, we're considering as many as fifty possible suspects. That's a lot of people to investigate."

The professor rubbed his large hands together, the scraping of skin against skin loud. "Then it is most fortunate that we have almost two weeks before we reach Cairo. Plenty of time to carry out our research. Plenty, indeed. Isn't this the most delightful trip you could've imagined?"

I closed my eyes briefly and wondered when I'd be able to resume my medication. "Actually, the most delightful trip I could imagine is one in which I have room service and never have to leave my cabin."

"Magnificent." He clapped his hands loudly enough for passengers near us to glance over with judgmental frowns. "We are in agreement, then. We launch our investigation this very morning, right after breakfast, as soon as possible."

I rubbed my temples, then waved at a waiter

and pointed to the teapot. At this rate, I could only hope that Chief Steward Stewart had the galleys well stocked with tea leaves.

Chapter Nine

I returned to my cabin as soon as was socially appropriate. That took far longer than expected, for Captain McCormick expressed interest in chatting with us beyond what decent manners required. And I could hardly give an excuse that I needed to launch my investigation. As far as the captain, his crew and the other passengers were concerned, I was the innocent, unassuming niece of a professor of English.

Such an infuriating disguise to maintain, I thought as I smiled at the captain's comment regarding the approaching storm and a promise of sunshine afterward.

"And my deepest apologies once again for the

intrusion into your cabin," the captain said for the umpteenth time.

I tried not to grit my teeth. "I'm not sure I would refer to it as an intrusion—"

"Quite right, miss. It was more of a mistaken entrance," the captain said. "Another passenger who had imbibed too much of the spirits and mistook your door for his. It shouldn't happen again."

"I'm sure it won't," I said, giving up on the pursuit of truth. There was no point in startling the good captain with my intentions of ensuring — by brute force, if necessary — that the intrusion would never happen again.

But back to my cabin.

I sagged against the door, then gasped when a ghost floated through the wall to one side of me.

"Gideon," I hissed.

"At your service, my beloved," he said and performed an elaborate but possibly sarcastic bow.

"In the future, please open the door and walk through the entrance like a civilized person."

"How dare you accuse me of being civilized."

"Don't be ridiculous, Gideon. I'd never accuse you of that. But we must still uphold a pretense of basic manners."

"Why should we do that, my love?"

It appeared death not only deprived one of a body but also of a sense of decorum. It was appalling, really. What was a widow to do?

"It's one thing to float through walls when one is alive," I lectured. "That would be considered a miracle. But to float through them when one is dead is quite unacceptable."

"Why?"

"Really, Gideon. I shouldn't have to explain this."

"Yet it seems you do."

"It's bad enough you've lost your body. Now to lose your manners on top of that? It's unacceptable. Death is no excuse for rudeness."

He shrugged and pirouetted upward until he was floating around the ceiling.

"So it was you in the dining room," I said.

"I wanted to ensure you had a good breakfast, so we could converse about our future without your normal morning grumpiness."

"I am *not* grumpy in the morning," I snapped and tossed my walking stick onto the bed. "But you, sir. Floating through walls. Spying on me while I try to enjoy my breakfast. Truly, it's more than a widow can endure."

"My apologies, darling." He floated down to my level and winked. "So if you're not too grumpy—"

"Of course not. I'm never in a foul mood. But I cannot tolerate this business of you haunting me. It's a bad habit you've adopted."

"Yes, and I would prefer that we return home as soon as possible."

I sat on the chair and stared at him. "And which home is that?"

He whirled a hand gracefully over his head. "It doesn't really matter which one. Although I don't see why we can't live in our old home as we did before."

"Because I am a widow, Gideon. As such, I don't have the means to maintain that household. And unless I'm a widow of sufficient wealth, which I'm not, it would be inappropriate for me to remain alone. People would wonder how I supported myself."

Gideon glanced up at the ceiling, as if studying the sky for inspiration. "Who cares what others think? As long as we're together—"

"I hate to break this to you, Gideon, but you're dead. So please move along."

Even as the words left my throat, I yearned to

drag them back down into the bowels from which they had ushered forth. For truth be told, I was glad to see him again, even if he was without a body. One can't expect everything from one's marriage partner.

"So are you with that foul family of yours? The Stewards?"

"I am, and I don't think Mrs. Steward would appreciate being haunted."

"I have no intention of haunting her, only you. So tell the captain to turn the ship around—"

"Out of the question, Gideon. The professor and I are on a mission. And it's of utmost importance we arrive in Cairo."

He threw up his arms in disbelief. "Really. You and your missions. I never understood how a young woman could be so independently minded as to pursue a career outside the home. Of course, that's also why I married you. You are a peculiar person, my dear Mrs. Knight."

"And you, sir, are a husband without a body and therefore of little use to anyone."

He grinned, and it was a grin full of mischief and mayhem. "Speaking of useful, did you see that cat?"

I sat on the chair, took out my notebook and

began making notes about the trip thus far. "Yes, it belongs to the captain."

"It's black."

"So I noticed."

"What was the captain thinking, bringing that beast aboard?"

"I believe he wanted to keep the ship rat-free."

"Black cats are bad luck."

"Says the ghost."

"Rub it in, why don't you? Can I ask you one favor?"

"No."

"Please?"

"Do I have a choice?"

"Not really. Please don't die at sea."

My heart softened at his appeal. "That's an easy favor, as I have no intention of doing so."

"What a relief. Because if you die here, I won't be able to go home. I'm stuck to you, you see. And I'd rather not be stuck while at the bottom of the ocean. It would be a tragic waste of a beautiful spirit."

"In that case, I'll do my best not to drown out here."

"That's all I ask." And with another rascally bow, he faded out of sight.

I sighed and rummaged through my valise for my ink bottle. While Prof. Runal and I hadn't discussed a plan of action, I'd already formulated one by the time I had arrived back at my cabin. I was reluctant to do it, but the first step involved squinting at each and every person on the ship. I hoped my late-night intruder was a normal human, but suspected otherwise. For who else would know about the importance of the toy pyramid except those who were opposed to the Society's agenda?

I needed to eliminate the risk of any para-normal element interfering with our mission. And so I finished my notes, put on my spectacles and prepared myself for a day of squinting.

Chapter Ten

I launched my investigation with a promenade around the first-class deck. As breakfast was finished, I hoped to identify most of my fellow passengers in this way.

In particular, I was curious about the odd couple who claimed to be siblings and sat in a corner table away from everyone else. Why did they keep casting strange looks in my direction?

It seemed the fates were against me, for they were not out and about. Instead, a jolly couple greeted me as I stepped onto the deck. She was as plump as he was thin. He was reserved while she was boisterous and sociable.

"Forgive my forwardness," the lady said, her

cheeks red with the blustery sea breeze. "I can't help but notice you are unaccompanied. Perhaps you would like to join myself and Mr. Spratt."

I pushed my energy-enhancing spectacles up my nose, glanced at their energy fields and politely smiled, but not too enthusiastically. An enthusiastic smile was far too encouraging of unwanted attention and awkward social interaction.

"That is most kind of you," I said, "but my uncle is expecting me to join him."

"Aha! So that's who it was," Mrs. Spratt said and elbowed her scrawny husband. "I told you there was nothing untoward occurring on *this* ship. I have sailed with Captain McCormick and his crew previously. They wouldn't allow such unbecoming behavior under their command."

Mr. Spratt shrugged, his skinny shoulders barely lifting his jacket.

"Nonetheless, my dear, join us," Mrs. Spratt said. "A bit of fresh air as we circumambulate the ship is most helpful and agreeable in assisting with digestion. Wouldn't you agree?"

As I wasn't keen to disclose my lack of digestive issues in public, I tipped my head in agreement with her invitation. As I did so, I focused my squint on the two Spratts. Their energy fields floated up around them. Purely human, holding nothing of interest and quite innocent of any nefarious intentions.

I sighed, unsure whether I should be disappointed or relieved. "I suppose one round of the deck would be quite acceptable while I wait for my uncle to join us. I'm Miss Knight."

"Delighted," Mrs. Spratt said and looped her arm with mine.

On that agreeable note, we set off. Mrs. Spratt was keen to inform me about all things British, most of which I had little or no interest in. By the time we had completed one circuit, I was updated on the affairs of Queen Victoria, the parliament, the latest fashion trends, the winning horse in yesterday's races, and the war being waged between the British Empire, its Egyptian allies and the Sudanese.

"It's quite unacceptable, how these people rebel against the very forces that bring civilization to their savage shores," she finished her monologue.

I glanced at Mr. Spratt, who had said not one word the entire time. Nor, I imagined, would he speak in the presence of his wife. She was a domineering figure both in physique and in dialogue.

"Perhaps they were content with their lives before the introduction of English fashion," I suggested.

"Nonsense," the good woman declared. "They simply didn't know what was good for them."

I pursed my lips. "You do remind me very greatly of my aunt."

"The flattering remark is well received, my dear Miss Knight," Mrs. Spratt said, her cheeks blushing with exertion at my apparent compliment.

At that moment, motion at the corner of my vision attracted my attention. A line heavy with tablecloths bounced from recent activity even though no one was near it, and it was shielded from the wind.

"I do believe I should go check on my uncle now," I said and disentangled my elbow from Mrs. Spratt's grip. "It's been a pleasure. Truly. Until next we meet." And before the woman could latch her verbal claws on me, I ducked away, walking in the opposite direction, toward the clothesline.

I squinted as I approached several crates tied down along one edge of the deck. The energy form that appeared was again of a human. I sighed but approached the person anyways, because who scuttled about with such secrecy except someone with a secret to keep?

I was again disappointed. A young sailor, a boy more than a man, was sitting in the shadows of the crates. He glanced up, his face scrunched in fearful concern, when I stood before him.

"You won't be telling, will you?" the young sailor asked, his voice high-pitched and trembling.

"Tell who what?"

The sailor stood, confirming my original appraisal of his youthfulness. I continued to squint, because I could see a lie of some sort weaving its way through his energy field. It was a significant lie alongside something else that didn't quite make sense.

"You didn't see, then?"

I stopped squinting to frown at the young man. "Goodness, do stop speaking in riddles. I didn't see what?"

"Nothing. Nothing at all. The name's Jack Clark."

"As I didn't request your name and have no reason to make your acquaintance, there's no need to tell me."

Sailor Clark nodded, still not meeting my gaze. "It's all good, then."

"I wouldn't go that far. Just last night, someone attempted to break into my cabin. You wouldn't know anything about that, now would you, young Clark?" I squinted at him, ready to pounce if I should see a hint of deception in his answer.

He looked up at me, his eyes large and startled. "Oh, no, miss. I'm not that sort. I swear."

He was telling the truth about his *sort*, whatever that might be. So what was his lie? What secret was he hiding?

"Your clothes are a tad big for you, aren't they?" I gestured to the oversized shirt that almost reached his knees.

"It's all that was available."

"That's a rather strange state of affairs."

Sailor Clark stared at my feet and said nothing. I gave up and left the boy to his own devices. I had concerns more important than oversized uniforms.

I continued to wander around the deck, then down to the dining room where midmorning tea was being served. So far, no one I'd met — neither passengers nor crew — had a suggestion of paranormal energy or violent intent. I was therefore surrounded by normal humans who were innocent of the unforgivable crime of disturbing my slumber.

Perhaps my original impression of the intruder

was incorrect. After all, I'd been half asleep, blurry-eyed and recovering from back-to-back nightmares.

Prof. Runal was sitting at our table. He waved at me with such enthusiasm he almost knocked the tray out of a passing waiter's hands. The only reason I could see to be enthusiastic was that a large pot of tea squatted in the middle of our table, surrounded by scones and biscuits.

"How goes the investigation, Beatrice?" Prof. Runal asked, his voice too loud for discretion's sake.

I gestured at him to lower his voice and glanced around. "Nothing so far, sir. Are you sure we shouldn't explore steerage?"

"Not yet, my dear. It's highly unlikely our culprit lurks down there, and I would spare you the assault on your senses if at all possible. But I have a plan. A scheme, as it were."

I immediately waved to a waiter and indicated that he should bring another teapot. When it came to Prof. Runal and his plans, significant quantities of some liquid or other were required to strengthen my nerves.

Prof. Runal leaned his elbows on the table, almost tipping it over in the process. Cups and saucers rattled in protest. "You see, Beatrice, it seems not all the passengers are present and accounted for at mealtimes."

I squeezed the bridge of my nose where the spectacles had left an indent. "And why would you think that?"

He bent closer, his heavy forearms pressing against the table. "When I booked these tickets, I was told quite clearly that we had purchased the last cabins available in first class. And yet I've seen a few chairs empty when they should really be occupied. Last night, this morning and even now."

"Maybe these are extras."

"No, not at all. We have thirty cabins in first class, and thirty chairs here, of which three have remained quite abandoned. This suggests there are a few passengers who haven't left their rooms. Now why would that be, Beatrice, dear? Pray tell me, why?"

I tightened the pinch on the bridge of my nose, hoping the slight discomfort would distract me from the direction I knew Prof. Runal was heading. "Because they're seasick?"

"Poppycock! Balderdash! We need to find out who exactly is on this ship. And do you know how we're going to do that, Beatrice?"

"I fear I do," I murmured and left my nose alone.

"Exactly. Then we are agreed!"

"About what?"

He tapped the side of his nose. "We are going to break into the captain's office and steal the passenger manifest."

Chapter Eleven

I took a few sips to strengthen my nerves before looking into the professor's deep brown eyes. "For a moment, sir, I thought you said you wanted us to *steal* the ship's passenger manifest. But surely I'm mistaken, as no one in their right mind would propose such a cockamamy plan."

"Gracious! Are you suggesting I'm in a *right* mind?"

"Of course not, sir."

"I'm glad to hear it."

I exhaled loudly. "So I misheard—"

"Not at all, Beatrice, not at all!" Prof. Runal thumped back in his chair. The unfortunate piece of furniture creaked and groaned in protest at his weight. "That's exactly what I want us to do. And by *us*, I mean *you*. For how else will we know the exact number and condition of our fellow passengers without it? How indeed!"

"I feared that's what you said."

"There is absolutely no need for fear, Beatrice. In fact, fears are no more use here, none at all! We shall remove the manifest and return it before anyone knows anything is amiss."

"Or we could just visit each and every cabin for ourselves."

"That's far too tedious a chore, Beatrice. Too long and involved. And we have little time to waste."

"We have almost two weeks."

"During which we must identify all possible suspects, then investigate each one thoroughly. And by thoroughly, I mean our mission will most likely involve breaking into their cabins, pilfering their supplies, and so on."

I didn't dare ask what *and so on* might refer to, as I'd worked with Prof. Runal long enough to divine his intentions. More importantly, I was too busy recovering from the notion that I would have to steal the captain's manifest. I focused on the tea, which despite the conditions of ship life was remarkably decent.

"Remind me to commend the captain on his selection of tea leaves," I said.

"Precisely right, Beatrice. This man knows his business, there's no doubt about it. After all, what's the point in being stranded on a ship in the company of normal humans without a good and steady supply of tea? None, that's what! Now, when shall we begin?"

"As you wish, sir."

"Excellent. We shall soon have a proper list from which to extract names and interrogate those with suspicious backgrounds and motives."

Meanwhile, the couple who had first attracted my attention — Lord Voleur and Lady Larrona — strolled into the dining room. Lady Larrona had changed into another stylish outfit but was still wearing her red feather boa and heavily feathered black hat.

Lord Voleur had replaced his top hat with a jaunty cap that matched his knowing smirk. He glanced around the room as if searching for something. His gaze lingered on me, and I stiffened my backbone so that I wouldn't squirm under his unappealing study. When I made no move to break eye contact, his smirk widened before he joined his female companion at the far table.

"What do you make of that couple over there, sir?" I asked in a low voice and hoped Prof. Runal would follow my example of discretion.

Alas, my hopes were dashed when he swiveled in his chair and blatantly stared at the far corner. "That stylishly dressed pair of siblings? Why, nothing at all, Beatrice. Not a bit. Indeed, they smell perfectly normal. Disappointingly so, considering their excellent taste in fashion. Now, let's go steal the manifest, shall we?"

There wasn't enough tea on board to strengthen my spirit for the task. And the pills in my pocket were not an option if we had any chance of completing this mission while successfully avoiding detection.

But one thing did speed up my heart and push energy through my sluggish limbs. Just at that moment, a ghostly form floated through a wall, gave me a dashing bow and pirouetted up through the ceiling. Despite the atrocious lack of manners which he exhibited, I was glad to have him here.

I was still smiling as I followed the professor out of the dining room and down a few flights of stairs to the level of the crew's quarters. Only when he led the way down a corridor narrower, darker and danker than the first-class corridor did I snap out of my reverie.

"Where would the captain keep the manifest?" I asked, wondering if Gideon would stay with me for the entire trip. The thought was mildly titillating, although I still intended to remind him to refrain from floating through walls and appearing so dramatically in my room.

"I suspect in his quarters, of course."

All thoughts of Gideon vanished. I stared at the professor's broad back in dull disbelief. "But you said we're going to his office."

"The captain's quarters usually double as his office, given the limits of space on a ship. I suspect that's where he keeps all things of value and interest."

"Do you mean to suggest ..." I gulped, my voice fading into a whimper of mild despair.

"That's exactly what I'm suggesting. Why the concern?"

"It's his private room."

"All the better!" The professor's voice boomed down the length of the corridor and echoed back at us. He was either oblivious of — or willfully ignoring — the need for stealth. "He shan't be there at this time of day. You'll break into his quarters while I keep a lookout. It shall be the quickest of jobs. You do remember your lessons regarding lock picking, do you not, Beatrice? We went over this numerous times during your training. I recall you were quite an apt student."

"Yes, I'm quite familiar with the ways and means to open a lock without a key. However—"

"Excellent! Magnificent! You always were a brilliant student. So you see there's no reason not to proceed."

"Apart from the fact it's illegal—"

"Humans and their silly rules."

"And if we're caught—"

"We won't be."

"We'll spend the rest of the trip in the brig."

"A minor inconvenience." He stopped and looked over his shoulder at me. "But really! Miss Beatrice Knight, you're making quite an unseemly fuss over nothing. What could possibly go wrong?"

Rather than tempt the fates with a long list of all the things that could possibly go wrong while breaking into the captain's quarters, I shook my head and gestured for the professor to lead the way.

He positively beamed at my acquiescence. "That's the spirit! We'll have this done in a jiffy. In and out, so to speak. They won't even notice a thing."

The more he spoke on the matter, the more certain I was that this would be anything but a quick and easy job. Nonetheless, I followed him through a network of ever-narrowing corridors to the far end of the ship.

Straight ahead, at the end of the last hallway, was a door upon which a metal plaque announced, "Captain's quarters." Underneath it was another sign with a statement which declared, "Do not disturb. Trespassers will be prosecuted."

Chapter Twelve

I read the second sign aloud, in case Prof. Runal hadn't noticed it. "Do not disturb. Trespassers will be prosecuted."

"Hardly welcoming, is it?" Prof. Runal said and chuckled.

I glanced around. There were several other doors along this section of the crew's level, each with a metal plaque. Chief Engineer. Chief Steward. Chief Officer. All the senior crew were housed together. I silently prayed they were all thoroughly occupied with the day-to-day running of the ship to pop down here for a nap or a nip of something.

"Beatrice, my dear, I shall stand right here while you proceed."

I stared at him. The space in which we stood

was so narrow, I would need to squeeze to get past him. There was no place to hide. "Here? In the middle of a corridor in the senior crew's section? And what excuse will you give if anyone should wander down here?"

"Quite right. Perhaps I shall keep watch at the intersection." He gestured vaguely in the direction from which we came.

"And again, what excuse will you provide?"

"I'm searching for the ship's doctor, of course. Something in the breakfast has ailed me terribly. Or perhaps it's the rocking motion of the ship. Why, I believe I'm seasick."

I shook my head and wished I had such an excuse. Sadly, my stomach was immune to all forms of illness. "We've had nothing but smooth ocean since we left. You're more likely to experience seasickness while riding a horse than being on this ship."

"Food poisoning it is. Very well. Off you go."

"And what signal will we use if someone should come into this area?"

The old werewolf wrinkled his nose as if sniffing for the answer. "Let's see. What indeed … Aha! I shall groan vociferously and cough three times."

"And you think I shall hear that while inside the captain's quarters?"

"I shall do so particularly loudly, exceptionally so. Let's stop thinking up problems, shall we?" With that, the professor squeezed past me and trundled down the corridor, his large shoes falling heavily against the flooring.

"I certainly hope they serve tea in the brig," I muttered to his back before turning to the work at hand.

A tap on a button on my walking stick released a trigger. A small drawer slid out, revealing my lock pick set. The captain's door was secured with a fairly simple mechanism. Clearly the man hadn't expected anyone to attempt to break into his quarters. Otherwise, he would've installed a more sophisticated lock. Not that I was complaining. I was quite grateful for the relative level of trust exhibited by the captain. Grateful and a tad bit guilty that I was about to break it.

"But we shall return the manifest promptly," I whispered reassurances to myself.

The lock opened with a sharp *snick*, and I eased the door ajar, just enough to slip through before closing it behind me. The captain's quarters weren't much bigger than my own. On one side was the sleeping area with a narrow bed. A steamer trunk rested underneath, a convenient storage for clothes and other personal items.

On the other side of the room was an office setup: a wooden desk that looked like it had seen its fair share of adventures at sea; a small shelf above it with several sailing-related books. A piece of equipment grabbed my interest, and I hurried forward to get a closer look.

It was a sextant, its coppery surface perfectly polished. It reminded me of a similar-looking instrument that the Society used from time to time to identify constellations of supernatural activity in a geographical area. Sadly, this one before me was of a more mundane nature, only useful for measuring the angle between the stars and the horizon as part of celestial navigation. Still, it was a beautiful piece of equipment.

Something moved at the far end of the room, and I spun around, half-expecting to see Gideon floating before me. But it was the black cat named Cairo. It was curled up on the ledge underneath a large, circular window, basking in a weak ray of watery sunlight. It blinked its eyes sleepily at me before stretching and arching its back. Then, with the whisk of its tail, it gracefully leaped off the sill, padded toward me and wrapped itself around my boots, purring loudly.

"You'll have to keep it down, Cairo," I said as I focused myself on the task.

The cat purred agreeably and returned to its sill, where it curled up and promptly fell back asleep.

"Lucky feline," I said and began opening and closing drawers in the desk.

The third one revealed a journal, its dark-brown leather surface stained with sea salt and years of use. I paused, listening for any sound of a cough. There was none, so I retrieved the journal and opened it to the front page. Written in block letters were the words I'd hoped to read: S.S. *Suez* Passenger Manifest.

"It seems the good professor was correct," I said. "As easy as any mission has ever—"

Cough.

I tensed and regretted having spoken so soon. I held my breath and waited to see if the cough would repeat.

Cough! Cough! … Cough, cough, cough!

"A pox on a werewolf's schemes."

Couldn't anyone follow a simple schedule these days? Shouldn't the captain be captaining or whatever it was called? I quietly closed the drawer, slid the journal into my purse next to the pyramid and tiptoed to the door.

I pressed my ear against the wood and listened for the sounds of an argument or struggle. At first, I could only hear the hull creaking under its load, the bellow of the ship's engines, distant footsteps, and gentle waves sloshing against the ship. The sounds echoed around me, distorting my sense of direction. And then, a voice slipped under the door.

"Oi! This here is off limits to passengers, sir."

It was the chief engineer, or Rocky as his fellow sailors referred to him. His thick Scottish accent cut through all other background noises.

Prof. Runal chuckled, his hearty guffaw reaching me as clearly as if he were standing on the other side of the door. "An honest mistake, sir. Truly, such mistakes do happen. I suppose I was a bit turned around. I'm looking for the tearoom."

"We have no tearoom, sir. Only the dining room, and midmorning tea has already been served. You'll have to wait until lunchtime."

"Quite right, sir. Quite right, I shall. Perhaps you could guide me out of this maze? It's quite confusing, all of these interlinking passageways and such."

"Hardly, sir. Just walk straight down that one there, and you'll reach a set of stairs. Up you go, and you'll see first-class quarters are there along with a door to the deck. Straightforward, mind you."

"Yes, but I was actually hoping to find the ship's doctor."

I slapped a hand on my forehead. The professor was usually adept at keeping his stories straight, but he seemed to be confusing both his listener and himself.

"I thought you wanted tea?" Rocky asked.

"Tea being the miracle drink that it is, it does settle an uneasy stomach, my dear engineer, so that's what I wanted. But as there is none, I shall have to request the ship doctor. We do have a ship doctor, don't we? Oh, tell me we do."

Rocky huffed. "'Course we do. Come with me, then. And make haste. I do have other work to do. I'm an engineer, not a tour guide."

"So true, sir. How very accurate indeed."

I waited a minute, then another until I was certain they had left the intersection. As I wasn't as certain where the medical office was, I decided not to delay any more and started to ease open the door.

"Keep an eye on them," a man said a stone's throw from the captain's door.

I froze, my hand still on the doorknob. Chief Engineer Rocky's accent was distinct enough to leave no doubt he had returned with great haste from the medical office.

"Aye aye, sir," a gruff voice I didn't recognize replied. It sounded like the man was chewing on gravel. "Suspicious pair, ain't they?"

"That they are, lad. Off you go," Rocky said.

How did I not hear those two approaching? The medical office must be close by for Rocky to have returned so quickly. As for the other man, he must be light on his feet. Or perhaps the ship's various background noises had obscured the sound of their movements. Still, that was a poor excuse. I was usually more attentive than this. Prof. Runal would be so disappointed.

But all thoughts of the professor and his displeasure disappeared when the doorknob underneath my hand began to turn. Without thinking, I reached over and flipped the lock around, hoping the man on the other side couldn't hear the soft *snick* it made as it fell into place.

The doorknob completed its turn, and the chief

engineer pushed on the door, then rattled it. "Blast it."

I waited for him to leave. But still I couldn't hear his footsteps. I glanced around the room, meeting Cairo's yellow gaze. It yawned, exposing its small fangs.

I waited for a count of ten. And just before I made the decision to open the door and take the risk, a key jingled in the lock.

Chapter Thirteen

I backed away from the door. Now what?

"You should hide in the closet," someone whispered behind me.

I jumped around and almost screamed as the cat stood up and stretched.

"You talk?" I whispered.

"Of course. Just try to stop me."

Gideon shimmered into view and waved his fingers. He was sitting next to the cat, his image faded from the light streaming in from behind and through him. He gestured to a narrow closet. "There should be room in there. Just try not to breathe."

I didn't have time to reconsider. Three long strides, and I opened the closet and slid in between the captain's spare uniform and a long, heavy rain jacket. The confined space stunk of mothballs. I'd just closed the door when the other door slammed open, and someone marched into the room.

"You're breathing."

I glared at the wood pressed against my nose but dared not speak back to Gideon. I only hoped that Chief Engineer Rocky couldn't hear or see ghosts. Otherwise, Rocky would open the closet to investigate, and how would I explain my presence in here?

"Now where did it go?" Rocky muttered and cursed under his breath — most creatively, I must say — while rummaging through the desk drawers. He opened one after the other in quick succession and slammed them shut in frustration.

The passenger manifest seemed to gain weight in my bag, and I held my breath.

"Much better, Beatrice," Gideon whispered. "Breathing is so overrated, isn't it?"

The man must've given up on the desk, for the scraping of the heavy steamer trunk being dragged across the floor filled the room.

"Of course it's locked. That man trusts no one. What does he think? I'm an engineer, not a thief, blast it all."

More scraping as the trunk was pushed, presumably back under the bed. A moment later, the door slammed shut, and the lock turned.

I exhaled loudly. "Gideon, make yourself useful and see if there's anyone in the corridor."

"That means I have to float through the door."

"So?"

Gideon's form began to shine brightly in the small closet. "I believe you mentioned it was the height of ill manners to float through solid substances such as doors and walls. And you know how important good manners are to me, not to mention your good thoughts about me."

"Oh, you are a difficult and tiresome creature."

"Say the word, and I shall float through any substance you request."

I opened the closet door and stumbled out, breathing in deeply. My head felt dizzy from inhaling whatever chemicals mothballs exude. "A pox on manners. Float through that door and tell me if it's clear."

The rascal grinned and did an elaborate bow before skipping through the door and out of the room. I waited for a moment, expecting him to pop back in. But he didn't.

"I knew I should've resigned," I told Cairo. "A

pox on males, human and otherwise. Gideon …
Gideon! Is there anyone else out there?"

Gideon thrust his head through the door and
stared at me. Behind me, the cat hissed.

"You didn't say anything about me coming back
in and reporting," he said.

"It was implied. And do come in. It's rather
disconcerting seeing a head sticking out of a door as
if it's a hunting trophy."

"It's all clear," he said and retracted his head.

I opened the door cautiously, just in case my
ghostly husband was inattentive to details. One
never knew with ghosts. Their perception of reality
changed once they lost their body.

But the corridor was empty, although not for
long. I could hear voices approaching from a distant
corner. I slipped out, closed the door behind me
and hurried down the corridor, already making my
excuses in case anyone found me here.

And I almost made it, having reached the intersection with the passage leading to the stairs, when I
ran straight into a sailor. We bounced off each
other and collapsed against opposite walls where we
stared at each other.

"Fancy meeting you here, Sailor Clark," I said,
and paused. Standing this close to each other, the

strangeness of the sailor's energy suddenly made sense. "Although I suspect *Jack* might stand for Jacklyn."

The young sailor gasped, and the sound took on a more feminine aspect as he — or rather she — sobbed once. She then straightened and gave me a look as if daring me to prove she was anything but a regular sailor. "I don't know what you're talking about, miss, but you shouldn't be in this part of the ship."

"Neither should you, I daresay," I said and brushed invisible dust off of my skirt. "You needn't worry, Jacklyn, or whatever your name really is. Your secret is quite safe with me."

The sailor gave up the pretense, her shoulders slouching in defeat. "The name's Eleanor Keene. And you really won't tell anyone?"

"I see no reason for me to interfere in what is clearly none of my business. Although I can't imagine why any female would want to associate with a crew of minimally washed males. It's hardly the life I imagine any woman would want."

Then again, I thought, many would say the same about my lifestyle choices.

Eleanor wiped a sleeve under her nose. "And why should adventures only be the domain of men?

Do women not have hearts as equally stout and fierce as any man?"

"Fierce, most likely. As for stout, neither one of us fits that description." I smiled to soften my words, for I decided there and then that Eleanor Keene was in fact quite a remarkable young lady.

"I'm fierce," she said, then studied her shoes. "My father was deciding whether to marry me off to the neighbor or send me to a monastery. I'm the youngest of a dozen children, and there's only so much our farm can feed."

"Was the neighbor so unappealing?"

She shuddered. "He was fifty at least, and I have no intention of marrying someone who's older than my own father."

"Quite right, my dear. Well, I do hope your adventures take you to a happier situation or at least a more appealing one."

She smiled, and I could clearly see her feminine attributes shining in that expression. "Oh, I shall. I intend to work my way onto a ship that's sailing for the New World. I'm sure out there, I shall have a much greater opportunity to set my own course, unhindered by family limitations."

"Indeed, one can only hope they are more liberated than our old-world society. Since I now know your secret, perhaps I can share one of mine."

She nodded eagerly.

"Someone broke into my cabin last night while I slept."

I waited for her gasp of horror before continuing. "I suspect the person or persons involved will try so again. Would you be kind enough to keep an ear out and let me know of any suspicious-sounding conversations or activities?"

Eleanor lifted her chin and nodded once. "It would be my pleasure. What will you do once you find the person?"

I liked her more and more. Her confidence that I would actually succeed in my quest softened my heart toward her. "Let me handle them."

"Will it involve making them walk the plank?"

"One can only hope."

On that agreeable note, we went our separate ways.

I hurried down the corridor, up the stairs and into the first-class dining room, where I found the professor waiting at our table. Lunch was not being served yet, but he had somehow convinced the waiter to bring a pot of tea.

"Success?" he asked the moment I sat down.

I tried not to scowl but couldn't avoid a slight frown. I'm sure Mrs. Steward would've been horrified if she had seen it. Then again, my current circumstances would've thrown her into a nervous fit serious enough to incapacitate her for the rest of the day.

"Yes, and no thanks to you. I was almost caught. Twice!"

"But you succeeded, as I knew you would," the professor said. "My faith in you has been confirmed again and again. So let's take a look."

"Here?"

"Do you see anyone around who might be suspicious? We can't very well meet in one of our cabins."

I quivered at the thought. That would seem far too suspicious, even for an uncle traveling with his niece. I pulled out the passenger manifest and laid it between us.

"Phenomenal. Tremendous! Let's read through the names and the cabin numbers, and you make a note of any that strike us as worthy of additional attention. We can then divide the list and systematically interrogate each and every one of them."

"You mean have a conversation with them."

"Exactly what I said. Are you ready?"

"There must be a couple hundred names on that list."

"We'll focus on first class and the crew."

"And it will be just our luck that the thief is hiding in steerage."

"Which would make it that much harder for us to interrogate him, or for him to repeat the exercise of breaking into one of our cabins," Prof. Runal said. "Now, are you quite ready?"

I gave up on persuasion and settled into writing the list of names and cabin numbers in my notebook. "I believe we can scratch Mr. and Mrs. Spratt from the list, along with Sailor Jack Clark."

"As you will, Beatrice. As you will. I have a theory that the crew in general is above suspicion, since the S.S. *Suez* was out at sea or at foreign ports for more than a couple of months until a few days ago, and I have been followed around for well over a week. Unless there are any new crewmembers?"

I scanned the crew listing. "All of them were aboard on the last trip except Sailor Jack Clark—"

"Whom you say is off the suspects' list."

"I am certain of that. There is also a sailor named Pip. No surname given. He's new to the crew."

"Perfect. Let's see if we can identify him without drawing attention to ourselves."

We continued in this way until we reached the end of the list.

"These three rooms here," the professor said, and tapped the lines in the manifest. "All three are occupied, one by a Mrs. Twitcher, one by Miss Devin, and the third … Most peculiar."

I looked up as a waiter passed by far too close for discretion's sake. "We need to finish up, sir."

"Yes, yes, my dear. We shall. We shall indeed. This third room says it's occupied, but no name has been given."

"Someone who values privacy?"

"And I can't blame the person for wanting it, not at all. But a passenger manifest must list each and every person by name. At any rate, the occupants of these three rooms have a comment added to their details. They have each requested to have all their meals delivered to their cabins. This seems suspicious, don't you think?"

"Indubitably. About as suspicious as the chocolate pudding."

Prof. Runal looked up. "What did the pudding do?"

"Nothing, sir. You were saying?"

"Just that, Beatrice. I suggest we target those three specifically. I shall leave them to you."

"To me?"

"Indeed. For two are female, which makes me suspect the unknown third passenger is also a woman. And it would hardly be appropriate for me to be knocking on their doors."

I sighed and stared at the list of thirty first-class passengers and twenty crewmembers. A good thing we weren't interviewing steerage passengers, as they numbered close to two hundred.

"Very well," I said. "I'll take the women, you take the men."

"Oh, no, my dear Beatrice. That will never do. Men are far more likely to provide information to a young, innocent-looking woman than to a hulk such as myself. They won't give me the time of day, unless we meet in the smoking room, and the stench of burning plant matter is reprehensible in close quarters."

All pretense that this was a holiday in the sun vanished as the professor laid out his plan. He would interview the senior crew while I focused on the first-class passengers who were either women or were accompanied by a woman. After some argument, he finally agreed to handle any passengers who were single males. I'd sift through the sailors to see which ones I could easily approach, and which ones I'd leave to him. That gave him a list of eleven, and twenty-three for me.

"This will take the full two weeks at this rate," I complained as we finished divvying up the list.

"Nonsense. Not at all. Take advantage of the tea breaks. That's when the formal sitting arrangements aren't quite so rigid. Oh, and the captain mentioned that he's organized a card game for the women tonight. Now that should be a fine opportunity indeed. Why, you can eliminate at least half your list in one go! I strongly encourage you to join that game."

And by encourage, he meant an order.

"What shall we do with the manifest?" I said as I closed it and tapped its cover.

Prof. Runal stared at me, his caterpillar eyebrows inching up his forehead in surprise. "Why, we must return it to the captain's quarters immediately, of course. Before he finds it missing. We can't have that, now can we?"

"Of course."

"And I shall leave it to your discretion, my dear, as I have an appointment with Chief Steward Stewart this very moment."

"But—"

The old werewolf tapped the side of his nose and waggled his hairy caterpillar eyebrows. "Then again, I needn't worry. That's quite a secret you have."

"What?" My hand fell to my jacket pocket and felt the outline of my pillbox.

"You shan't be alone, now shall you? What with Mr. Gideon Knight back at your side."

My shoulders sagged. "Of course, sir."

Chapter Fourteen

Returning the passenger manifest to its rightful owner wasn't nearly as fraught with danger as stealing it was. I sent Gideon ahead of me to scout out the passageways, but not before he pouted and made a show of how I abused him for his talents.

"You're treating me as if I'm little more than your personal scout," he said, his bottom lip poking out in a sulk. "This is not at all how I imagined our reunion to be."

I waved him ahead of me. "I'd rather we not discuss what you imagined."

He turned and floated backward so he could face me. Sighing, he placed a hand over his heart, or at least the location where his heart would've been had he had a body. "But I had such magnificent plans, my dear wife. Surely you want to hear them? It starts with—"

"Absolutely not. Because I'm sure whatever scheme you concocted is not entirely suitable for polite conversation."

"Of course it isn't," he said and snorted derisively. "Polite conversation is terribly overrated."

"Gideon, go search the corridors."

He spun around and sank through the closest wall. I believed he did that on purpose, knowing how I felt about that trick. There was only one thing worse than a rude ghost, and that was a messy corpse. Of course, running out of tea leaves would definitely make the top of the list of horrors I intended to avoid at all cost.

Gideon's head appeared out of the wall. "All clear."

I ignored his whispery laughter as I stalked down the corridor. It was a good thing I was returning the book, because I had neglected to lock the captain's door behind me in my rush to escape. I took great care to position the journal in the exact way I had found it. Closing the drawer carefully, I was about to exit the room when a voice shouted out, "Stop right there!"

I froze, hand on the doorknob.

"Now what is it?" Rocky asked. "I'm due for a break, and I intend to take it, blast it all."

"Sorry, sir. Captain needs you. One of the first-class passengers had a bit of an upset."

"What's it to me? I'm an engineer, not a doctor."

The first man chuckled. "Can't say, sir, but he asked for you."

The two walked away, exchanging good-natured banter about the stupidity of the passengers. Their overall consensus was the bigger the wallet, the smaller the brains, or something to that effect.

"It's all clear, in case you were wondering," Gideon said as he leaned through the door.

"You vex me, Gideon," I said. "You're doing this on purpose."

He opened his eyes wide in a mockery of innocence. "Who, me? How could I ever be a bother to my beloved wife? I'm simply doing as I was told. Keeping a lookout."

I locked the door this time and made it to the deck without any additional misadventures.

As the afternoon proceeded, I managed to cross off a few more names from my list. I glanced at the bottom three names, the mystery passengers who had yet to leave their rooms. If I was at all lucky, those three would be at the ladies' card game that evening. Then again, Lady Luck and I were not well acquainted. I wasn't sure what I did to offend her, but she tended to avoid my company.

Eventually, I tired of all the strolls I'd taken on deck and decided I'd earned a few hours of solitary confinement.

I'd seen no sign of the steerage passengers, which proved Prof. Runal's point. They had their own deck, albeit much smaller and closer to the waves, and never had reason or permission to ascend beyond that. I made a mental note to ask my new friend Eleanor Keene if she could provide me some information about those less fortunate individuals.

After dinner, I bade Prof. Runal good luck as he accompanied some of the men to the bar for drinks and manly discussions about polo and fashionable cravats, or whatever men discussed when alone. The waiters, under the keen eye of Chief Steward Stewart, rearranged the tables in the dining room until there were three large settings for the ladies to gather around. A waiter sat at each table with the cards before him.

Soon, all three tables were full of ladies clutching their cards and gossiping. More attention was paid to the gossip than the cards, as was evident by the mounting piles of chips in front of the card dealers. Obedient to Prof. Runal's requests, I circulated between all three tables, joining conversations whenever possible, squinting at each of the women in turn as I asked them innocent questions such as, "What does your husband or family do?" and, "Have you much interest in antiquities?"

Most of the women freely shared insipid responses, such that I immediately scratched their names off of the list. If they or their husbands were involved in anything more nefarious than ridiculous fashion, unhealthy diets and obscene gossip, then I was not seeing it.

As we entered our third round of games, Lady Larrona strolled into the room as if she owned it. And the way she was dressed, she very well might. She'd exchanged her feather boa for a fur wrap and stood on shoes so tall I marveled how she could maintain her balance. She kept her chin high so that she peered down her straight nose at everyone seated around the tables, as if she was far too superior to join us, the first-class rabble.

I waited for her to take a seat and was pleasantly surprised when she sat at my table, selecting a chair close to mine. She acknowledged none of us but held her hand out imperiously for a set of cards. The card dealer obliged, then set the bets.

"Exciting, isn't it?" I said to open the conversation as I leaned past the woman sitting between us and stared at her. No paranormal glimmer lit up her energy field, but she was by no means an innocent passenger.

She glanced at me, her lips quirking upward in a cruel smile. "If you say so. What business have you here?"

"I imagine the same as yours. A game of cards to pass the evening."

"Yes. One must entertain oneself as best one can, mustn't one?"

I smiled. "Indeed, one must. So what takes you to Cairo?"

"I have business interests. And you?"

"An educational tour with my uncle."

The woman sitting between us excused herself and retreated to the powder room. I used the opportunity to change seats.

"Is that what you young women call them these days," Lady Larrona said, her smile deepening into something bordering on wicked.

"Calling what?"

"Men with whom they are associated. In my days, we didn't refer to them as *uncle*."

A hot flush crept up my throat and flushed my cheeks. "I assure you, nothing of that nature is happening between myself and my uncle."

She waved a hand vaguely at me and clucked her tongue. "Now, now, young lady. There's no need for us to maintain the conventions of our restrictive society. We are in international waters and thus are free of any such male-imposed foolishness. But if you wish to maintain the pretense, then your uncle he shall be."

I snapped my mouth shut before I said anything else. Her gloating expression suggested she was trying to bait me. But why? I could think of only one response: she had her suspicions about me, just as I had about her.

"And would you look at that?" She laid down her cards. "I do believe I've won this round."

I nodded at her as she stood to leave. "Yes, it seems you have. But there are many more rounds ahead of us."

Chapter Fifteen

At breakfast, Prof. Runal inquired after my evening, then informed me he had conversed with several of the gentlemen passengers, none of whom seemed or smelled suspicious.

"But I did play cards with the captain," he added. "I hope he's a better sailor than a card player. He couldn't win a round if Lady Luck sat on his head."

"My, such an appealing image," I murmured.

I hastily finished my meal and retreated to my cabin with a pot of tea and my list. I wanted to refine my thoughts and identify the most likely villains.

I managed to eliminate most of the female first-class passengers and their husbands, brothers or uncles. But Lady Larrona, she of the red-feathered boa, had rapidly crept to the top of my suspect list. In addition, the three guests who had yet to leave their cabins were also on the short list.

It seemed Prof. Runal was correct: I would have to find some excuse with which to lure them out of their cabins, or encourage them to invite me in. Neither one of those prospects struck me as desirable. Necessary, yes. But I'd rather sit across from Lady Larrona and lose card games than intrude upon another's privacy.

There was also the new sailor Pip. I was fairly certain that my young Eleanor Keene, masquerading as a boy, was innocent of any crime apart from disguising her gender. But Pip was an unknown quantity. I decided to track him down and interview him first. If I was lucky, he'd be the culprit, and I could ignore the existence of the three privacy-seeking guests.

While I'm not one to talk excessively about the weather, in this case it played an important role. The ocean's calm surface was rapidly transforming as a heavy wind stirred the surface into a frothing madness. Waves of ever-increasing size slapped against the ship, buffeting it back and forth, while a cold dampness whistled across the deck. So much for our holiday in the sun.

As a result of the inclement weather, none of the other passengers dared venture outside for a promenade around the deck. Occasionally, a sailor would hustle past me, racing between one task and another. I decided to use the privacy created by the angry sky to get some fresh air while attempting to solve the pyramid's true purpose.

I found a quiet corner tucked behind one of the life rafts. I leaned against the small boat and stared across the railing at the white-capped waves.

"You aren't considering jumping, are you, Beatrice, love?" Gideon whispered as he manifested to one side of me.

"I almost did, you startled me so. I've already informed you how I detest this habit."

"Which one? Walking through walls? Appearing dramatically before you?"

"Both."

He chuckled and joined me in studying the ocean's surface. "Looks like we're heading toward a storm."

"And what would you know of the matters of ship-craft and sailing?"

He shrugged. "I know a great many things,

Beatrice. I'm more than just a pretty face, you know."

I kept my mouth firmly shut in case I impulsively said something that could land me into more trouble than I was already in. Instead, I pressed my back against the life raft and retrieved the small pyramid.

"That looks entertaining. What is it?"

I held the strangely shaped box in front of my face. "At a glance, it is little more than an ornament, although apparently it's the key to ending a war. I'm not entirely convinced on the matter. But Prof. Runal—"

"That old dog," Gideon said and pretended to spit over the railing.

"There's no need for foul behavior, Gideon. It's not his fault he stinks like a wet dog."

"I wasn't referring to his smell."

I didn't comment on the strange statement. I had enough experiences with ghosts to know how their thoughts started to stray into paranoia and fantasy. The separation of body and spirit did strange things to the mind.

"Your personal issues with the professor notwithstanding, I would like you to practice a certain degree of manners. Without manners, we are nothing better than animals."

Gideon smirked and winked. "My dear Beatrice, we *are* animals."

"Speak for yourself." I did my best to ignore his subsequent unsavory comment and studied the pyramid.

It was made of wood, but a type I'd never seen before. Its surface had a golden red sheen. The grain was so smooth, it felt more like silk than wood. It was a perfect replica of the Great Pyramid of Giza. I suspected that if I counted all of the small blocks, the number would be exactly the same as the original giant pyramid. That in itself showed great craftsmanship and an attention to detail I couldn't help but admire.

"I wonder how this replica is supposed to be a key," I said as I turned the pyramid around. "I can't imagine a keyhole the shape of a prism." My voice was snatched away by a heavy gust of wind, and I shivered.

"Beatrice, I don't want you dying of pneumonia," Gideon said. "Who would I haunt if you were gone? Perhaps you would do us both the favor of returning to the warmer interior?"

"A little bit of cold isn't going to kill me, Gideon."

He fussed and continued talking, but I was no longer paying any attention. I found several seams in the otherwise flawless pyramid. "A box, perhaps? Or … I do believe this is a puzzle."

"You're the puzzle," Gideon said.

"Perhaps there's literally a key inside of it, which would make more sense than the pyramid itself being the key. If I can open this puzzle, we can store its contents in a safer place."

"And which place would that be?"

I waved a hand at Gideon. "I could put it on a necklace and hide it under my shirt."

Gideon floated in front of me. "I should hope that's a very safe place indeed."

As I fiddled with the pyramid that was maybe a puzzle, something brushed against my legs. I'm not the squeamish sort, but I couldn't prevent a slight squeak and a jump which caused me to bump against the life raft.

Cairo sat by my boots, tail tucked neatly around its legs. It purred and slapped a paw against my boots.

"It looks like you have a new best friend," Gideon said. "Should I be jealous?"

"You're dead. Of course you shouldn't."

"There's no need to rub it in." His pout was the last thing to fade from view as he left me with the cat.

I bent down and stroked the animal. Its purr grew louder, and I smiled.

"I can see why people like to keep cats around. Apart from their useful function of removing rats from a ship, they are actually quite pleasant."

As if agreeing with me, Cairo rubbed its head against my hand, encouraging me to scratch behind its pointed ears.

After a few moments of mutual enjoyment, I focused again on the puzzle. "Perhaps if I try to twist it this way." Something clicked when I did. I paused and shook the pyramid. Nothing rattled. I could only hope I hadn't broken it.

"Fancy meeting you here, Miss Knight."

The cat arched its back, I instinctively thrust the pyramid under one armpit and crossed my arms over my chest as I straightened. Lady Larrona stood off to one side, watching me.

"Indeed. I find such weather bracing and invigorating," I said.

The woman smirked and glanced down at

Cairo. "I never could understand why anyone likes these vermin."

The cat hissed and darted away. I wished I could do the same.

"Would you care to join me on a circumambulation of the deck?" Lady Larrona asked, her gaze scanning me up and down as if searching for something.

"I shall have to decline your kind invitation this time. I've been out here longer than I expected, and I believe a cup of tea is in order. But you enjoy your stroll."

"A pity. Of all the female companions I could have, you strike me as one of the more intelligent and interesting ones."

"You compliment me too much. Perhaps we shall dine together at a later point."

"Perhaps we shall." She slowly spun around and sauntered away. I watched her go, frowning at her decision to investigate around the life raft. This was not a normal location for any passenger to loiter.

I was under no illusion. She didn't come out here in search of my company. So what had she been doing?

Chapter Sixteen

"I intend to break into the cabins of Lady Larrona and her companion Lord Voleur," I confided to Prof. Runal over lunch.

He chuckled as if I'd shared the most entertaining joke. "I admire your gumption, my dear. Truly a delight. What makes you believe they are suspects at all?"

"I can't imagine how they aren't. Do you not see them?" I tilted my head to the side. "Look at them! They're always bent over the table, conversing in strange whispers."

"As are we, it seems."

"I only wish you would whisper." I frowned at the professor.

His laugh bounced around the dining room,

causing heads to turn. "You needn't worry about them. Not that they are innocent of crime. Not at all. A suspicious couple, indeed. But I don't feel we need to concern ourselves with them, not when it comes to the pyramid."

"If you say so." My tone suggested I was anything but convinced.

"Have you been able to track down the elusive sailor Pip?"

"He's next on my list." I couldn't help but glance toward the far corner, catching Lady Larrona's smirking gaze.

"Jolly good, Beatrice." Prof. Runal clapped his hands and rubbed them vigorously. "I've managed to meet with most of the senior staff. A solid group, I must say."

"There was something strange about Rocky."

The professor's caterpillar eyebrows lifted upward. "What rock do you refer to, Beatrice?"

"Not a rock, sir. The chief engineer."

"Ah, yes. He has a charming nickname, if I recall."

"He's referred to as Rocky. He and one of the sailors seem to suspect two people of nefarious activities. And I'm wondering to whom they were referring."

"I'm sure I don't know."

"Could they mean us?"

Prof. Runal tipped back in his chair. The poor, spindly legs creaked in protest. I winced in anticipation, but they held the weight by some small miracle.

"Not possible, Beatrice. There's nothing at all suspicious about us, not a bit."

"Actually, sir——"

"At any rate, the chief engineer didn't greet my queries with any leeriness. But I suppose it doesn't hurt to keep an eye or two on him. Who was the other chap?"

"I'm not sure, but I'd recognize his voice. It was distinct."

"Excellent. Make a note of them, then."

I sighed and added Rocky and "sailor with gravelly voice" to the suspect list.

After lunch, we parted ways. I wandered around the deck and the corridors until by chance I met up with my new sailor friend, Eleanor, on the windy side of the deck.

"I need an introduction from you," I said as a way of greeting.

Eleanor glanced around, as if concerned anyone else would be out and about in the inclement weather. "I'm very much at the bottom of the hierarchy here, Miss Knight," she whispered.

"I suspect the person I want to see isn't much higher. A sailor named Pip."

Eleanor shuddered. "Oh, no, Miss Knight. You don't want to meet up with him."

"Your reaction confirms my intention and gives me hope. I very much desire to meet him. Is he dangerous?"

She nodded her head, her eyes wide with fear. "A scary fellow. He's huge and mean as well."

I smiled. "All the better, then. I must meet with him at once."

Eleanor whimpered. "You are a most peculiar woman, Miss Knight."

"Why, thank you. But your compliments are entirely unnecessary. Please escort me to Pip's work station."

"He's in the engine room right now, assisting Rocky. Or at least that's usually where he is. He doesn't leave that floor very often."

"Then to the engine room we shall proceed."

"But it's off limits."

"That only makes it more interesting. Point me in the direction, and I shall pretend I was looking for a powder room."

"Do you think they shall believe you mistook the *engine* room for a powder room?" my little sailor friend asked.

I chuckled. "Oh, my dear Eleanor. Men will believe anything when it comes to women, particularly if it reinforces their belief that women are the weaker and less intelligent member of the human species. I merely have to blink my eyes a few times, express shock and dismay at my current situation, and threaten to faint. Even the most hardened men will believe that I am capable of confusing a foul-smelling, loud engine room for something else."

"Really?"

"I swear it's true. However, we shall still use some discretion in case a kindhearted crewmember tries to redirect us. Now, let's proceed."

We scuttled through the corridors, going deeper into the bowels of the ship. Whenever anyone approached, we ducked into a room or behind a wall until the person — usually a sailor — passed us by. We very soon left all pretense of first-class lifestyle. The air became heavy and dank, the walls infused with the odor of men who spent too long at sea.

By the time the heavy *thunk* of the steam engine smothered all other sounds, I was wiping my forehead and yearning to return to the cool, breezy deck. Eleanor had to shout in order for me to hear her.

"There's the door, miss." She pointed straight ahead of us and quite unnecessarily, I must add.

A metal plaque clearly stated, "Engine Room. Crew Only." Below that was another sign: "Stay out. Dangerous machinery." In case anyone was illiterate, there was also a white palm inside a red circle.

"Thank you, Eleanor. I must admit that was easier than I anticipated. Disappointingly so."

Eleanor hesitated. "But it clearly says this is the engine room, and it's only for staff. How will you convince the men you're lost and confused?"

I patted her shoulder. "That part is a piece of cake. Leave it to me. Humans have a tendency to believe what they want to believe."

"Humans?"

"Huge men, of course. That's what I meant." Before she could interrogate me on my linguistic slip, I again thanked her for her assistance and hurried toward the door.

Chapter Seventeen

By the time I reached the door and its warning signs, Eleanor had abandoned me to my madness. It was for the best, as I could tell she wasn't nearly adept at the art of feminine manipulation as a young woman needed to be to survive in this world of men.

I'd thought it was deafening outside the room. My definition of noise changed dramatically the moment I opened the heavy door. A barrage of sound assaulted me, and my ears began to ring with the cacophony of mechanical works.

The clanks and thunks of heavy machinery, the hiss of steam, the relatively muted shout of a man communicating with another: all of it combined with the stench of oil and sweat. The sheer ferocity of it all overwhelmed my senses and almost persuaded me to abandon my mission.

Perhaps I could find sailor Pip in a more congenial location, I thought.

Instead, I pushed myself forward and closed the door behind me. There was no natural light in here, no windows to provide a glimpse of open ocean and clear skies. There was only darkness, stench and the clamor of the ship's heart. It took a moment for my eyesight to adjust, after which I followed the sound of men bellowing at each other.

I knew it was sailor Pip the moment I saw him. He was the only one I hadn't yet seen of all of the sailors. Perhaps the chief engineer kept him out of sight for a reason. And the reason was now very evident: the man was monstrous.

He was an equal match in stature to Prof. Runal, who was himself no small creature. Sailor Pip's arms were thicker than both of my thighs put together. His back was wide, heavily muscled and slightly hunched. As for his legs, I've seen smaller tree trunks. Numerous scars crisscrossed his features, as if battles had been fought across the surface of his face.

He was stripped to the waist, wearing only a dingy undershirt. Tattoos covered his exposed arms.

I squinted at him, but there was only human energy there. Still, that energy was intimidating enough.

No wonder Eleanor had warned me against meeting Pip.

Before I could decide to venture forward or retreat, the man straightened, rolled back his shoulders and turned. He held a wrench longer than my arm in one hand, and his face was furrowed into a stormy frown.

He glanced up when I took a step back, and his frown deepened. "What's you doin' here?" he yelled.

Although he shouted at me in order to be heard over the engine, he still sounded violently angry.

I tried blinking and smiling demurely, but my charms were lost in the shadowy lighting. So I tightened my grip on my walking stick. In my line of work, one does not simply wilt away at the sight of a physically superior specimen. My experience has proven to me that physical size has very little to do with prowess and the ability to win a fight. Nonetheless, I would be lying if I suggested I wasn't a tad bit alarmed. Still, the mission had to proceed.

"May I have a word, Mr. Pip?" I asked, maintaining a polite tone. Fear of dismemberment or other inconveniences was no excuse for poor manners.

"What?"

I cleared my throat and shouted back, "I have a question or two. Do you mind?" I indicated the door, which would provide an exit from the oppressive air.

He glanced around, as if searching for a reason to either ignore me or pummel me with the wrench. Finding none, he shrugged and slouched toward me. The deck rumbled with the force of the engine, but I was quite certain that if we were in any other location, the rumbling would be from the man's heavy boots crashing against the floorboards.

"Follow me," he grumbled loudly as he passed me.

I didn't argue. The moment we stepped into the corridor, I sighed in relief and sagged against the wall. The door sealed off the worst of the noise. Compared to the air in that room, out here was a sweet breath of spring.

"What does you want?" Pip asked in his distinct gravelly voice. He was the unknown sailor who had shared suspicions with the chief engineer about a couple of the passengers.

I glanced at his ragged features. He was even

more fearsome out here, now that I could see him clearly. He still clutched the wrench in one hand. With one swing, he could effortlessly knock me into oblivion. And then what would Gideon say? He had expressly forbidden me to die on this ship, not that he had anything to do with my decision to live or not.

I discreetly maneuvered my walking stick so I could lift it to block a blow. "I'm not sure if you heard, but someone broke into my cabin last night."

His ferocious expression didn't alter. He waited for me to continue rather than provide the socially acceptable murmur of sympathy or shock.

"And I'm attempting to discover if anyone has any information on the event." I paused and let the silence stretch between us.

Humans were notoriously uncomfortable with silence. At least, most humans were. If you kept quiet long enough, your conversational partner would jump into the emptiness of words and say something — anything — to fill the gap. And more often than not, what they said or didn't say communicated a significant amount.

Not so with sailor Pip. He remained unconcerned by the conversational void growing between us. He didn't move or so much as twitch in discomfort.

I exhaled heavily in frustration at his obstinate restraint. "So I was wondering if you perhaps knew anything about it."

"Why me?"

I didn't mean to, but my gaze dropped to the grotesque tattoos covering his arms. One in particular attracted my attention. While I was no expert on the ways of the sea, I suspected a skull and crossbones was not the sort of tattoo most sailors would select.

"That's an unusual image to permanently ink on one's arm," I said and tipped my head toward his left arm.

He covered the skull with a thick, heavy hand. "What of it?"

"None of the other sailors have it."

"So?"

Good grief. It was easier to extract blood from stone than an answer from this man. I decided to go ahead with my suspicion. "Were you once a pirate, Pip?"

Those words were a more potent key than my lock pick set. The hardened expression covering his heavily scarred face immediately crumbled into despair. He dropped the wrench, slapped his hands over his face and began to sob. His shoulders shook with the force of his tears.

"Oh, miss, please don't be tellin' no one. It's a horrid life. And I ain't proud of it. Not a bit. I barely escaped. And Rock's—"

"What rock?"

"The chief engineer. He's all heart. So generous. Ain't told no soul who I is, or where I comes from. But now you know!" With a wordless wail, he sank to the floor and hugged his bent legs, hiding his face behind his knees.

As intimidating and horrifying as he was before, this new side of the pirate presented me with a whole new level of terror. I stepped away from him, wondering what I should do now. Perhaps he wouldn't notice if I ran away.

"I swears I ain't got nothin' to do with it," Pip said, his voice hiccupping with the effort of saying more than three words in a sentence. "I swears, but not in front of you, miss. I'd never do nothin' like that. That's why Rocky, he keeps me here. Ain't got no cause to go up to the top deck. Not even to steerage. You asks him. Asks me bunkmates. Please don't tells the captain. They'll toss me off at the next port, and then them pirates, they'll finds me. And you knows what they do to pirates who abandon a pirate ship? Do you?"

I'd been gradually retreating during his rather lengthy and painful speech. I froze when he stopped ranting. He peered up at me, his face covered in tears. I risked another step backward, desperately wishing I had never descended to this place.

"I believe you. Truly. There's not a doubt in my mind. Now please stop crying, or I might be forced into a swoon in order to escape the extreme awkwardness of the situation."

In an effort to assist him, I rummaged around in my purse and removed an unused handkerchief. I fluttered the fabric in front of his face until he clutched it in one of his hands. The handkerchief almost disappeared inside that giant grasp.

"Thank you, miss. You's so kind. Truly all heart."

"I wouldn't go that far," I muttered.

"I ain't deservin' it. But thank you." He wiped the handkerchief across his face, smearing a dark, oily streak across the white fabric. He then blew his nose so noisily that I decided there and then he should keep the handkerchief.

"Do you have any idea who it could be, then?" I asked, almost not caring about his response. I simply wanted to escape this place and return to my cabin.

He shook his head. "No, miss. But if I finds that person, I'll toss him o'er the rails me self."

"While I deeply admire the sentiment, if not the actual deed, I'd prefer to question the suspect before we make him walk the plank."

After reassuring me that he wouldn't go to that extreme without my permission, I left him with the handkerchief and hurried upstairs for some fresh air.

Chapter Eighteen

That evening at dinner, I was saved from overindulging in pudding by an unusual invitation.

The plates from the main course had just been cleared, and I was eyeing the options for dessert. Creme caramel, chocolate cake or chocolate pudding. I glanced around and wondered if anyone apart from my stomach would notice if I indulged myself and ordered a plate of each. I'd feel the impact later that night, but sometimes sacrifices must be made for the greater good. And I could think of no greater good than two desserts involving chocolate.

Just then, one of the waiters approached and held out a silver tray, upon which lay a folded card. "For you, Miss Knight."

I exchanged surprised looks with Prof. Runal. Accepting the card, I opened it.

"This is most singular," I said as I quietly read the contents in the card.

"Well, then. Let's have it. Do tell!" Prof. Runal said and rubbed his hands.

I read it out loud: "I has info mashin—"

"What's a mashin?"

"I believe the writer meant *information*."

"That makes more sense. Carry on."

"Meet me in engine room. Quick. Alone. Your friend."

"Who could it be from?" the professor asked as I turned the card around in search of a signature.

"Based on the roughness of the penmanship, I suspect it's my new friend, pirate Pip."

The bushy caterpillar eyebrows crawled up the professor's wide forehead. "A pirate, no less? My, my. I must say I'm impressed by your natural ability to make acquaintances in all quarters. Impressed, indeed, my dear Beatrice."

"He was hardly a pirate. In fact, I'm amazed he's managed this long as a lowly sailor. But he did offer to toss my assailant over the railing if we should find him."

"Here, here," the professor said and lifted a

glass in a toast. "Pirates are a difficult lot of cutthroats, but make stalwart friends if they don't kill you first. I've known one or two in my time. Fine fellows, apart from their tendency to loot and pillage other ships. That's a minor inconvenience for such a fantastic and fascinating acquaintance."

"I quite concur, sir. And now, if you will please excuse me. There seems to be a certain urgency in the matter."

Prof. Runal nodded in agreement, then ordered two helpings of all the dessert options. I envied him, for he could do so without causing a stir amongst the waitstaff. If I were to order more than a half portion of anything, there would certainly be judgmental looks.

I buttoned up my jacket, slipped out of the dining room and hurried down the various levels to the bowels of the ship. The door was ajar when I reached the corridor to the engine room. The pounding of machinery echoed around me, magnified by the narrow confines.

Taking a last breath of relatively fresh air, I entered the room and closed the door behind me. The stench of oil and sweat clung to my skin and nostrils as if I'd been dipped in a puddle of the foul concoction.

"Pip?" I shouted.

A scuffling noise alerted me to the presence of another.

Perhaps this wasn't such a wise idea, after all, I thought.

Too late. The sense of a looming presence caused me to glance over my shoulder just as someone leaped out of the shadows. I staggered forward as the person's weight landed squarely on my back. Strong arms wrapped around my neck, and I fell heavily onto the slippery floor. My face landed in a puddle of oily water, and I gagged as some of it slipped across my lips and into my mouth.

Meanwhile, my arms were trapped beneath me along with my walking stick. My assailant kept one arm firmly around my neck, tightening, until I could barely breathe between the combination of oily water, fumes and the constriction against my throat.

I kicked my legs back and forth until my boots connected with a piece of machinery to one side. Using the leverage, I forced myself to roll over, dragging the assailant with me.

"Who's there?" a male voice shouted.

"Help!" I screamed, but my voice was frail with the pressure against my neck.

"Hello?"

Rather than waste energy on speech, I rolled and wrestled with my assailant. And just when I was about to gain the upper hand, he snatched my bag off my shoulder and kicked himself free of my grip. My assailant had already dashed away when pirate Pip appeared out of the noisy gloom and squatted next to me.

"Is you all right, miss? Did you slip? Do you needs a doc?"

He helped me sit up while I struggled to breathe. I kept shaking my head at his questions and gesturing toward the door.

"You wants air?" Before I could protest, the giant man scooped me up as if I was a child and lumbered toward the door. He yanked it open, stepped out into the corridor and let the door close softly behind him as he lowered me to the ground.

"Someone else," I gasped while trying to inhale deeply.

Pip's scarred face was now level with mine. "There be someone else needin' the doc?"

"No. The assailant. He was in there with me."

My dear pirate stood up with a cry and puffed

out his chest. "Is he? I'll knock 'im to bits. I'll toss 'im to the sharks. I'll—"

"He's gone."

"Oh." Pip deflated and sat down across from me. "I just missed 'im, then."

I nodded, my throat still raw from the fumes and my attacker's grip.

"You ain't hurt too bad, is you? What did he do?"

I shook my head and pulled out the invitation card. "Did you write this for me?"

Pip looked at his large, clunky boots and refused to take the card. "No, miss. Truth be told, I ain't got any learnin'. Can't write. Can't read, neither. Not even signs. Rocky showed me how to do everythin'. Good man, that one."

I opened up the card and stared at the rough, scrolling handwriting. "I'm sorry I thought it was you. And I'd hoped you had some information. That's what the invitation promised."

Pip rubbed his hand against his chin. "Sounds like a trap. He got you here on yer own. He ain't knowin' I stay late 'til the next shift comes. Or maybe he thought ain't no one around 'cause of dinner."

"Perhaps, which means whoever sent this isn't

familiar with the ship's schedule or the need to have someone in the engine room at all times."

Pip's eyes widened. "You's somethin' smart, miss. You read and write and that's very clever thinkin', too."

I smiled. The man's scarred face no longer seemed frightening. In fact, there was something almost tender about his eagerness and the compliments he bestowed upon me.

"What's this, now?"

We both stared up at the man looming over us. The only reason I hadn't noticed his approach was the noise and smell from the engine room.

Chief engineer Rocky McIntyre glared down at us. "Well, then? I've asked the question of the two of you. And I expect an answer."

"She's been attacked, sir," Pip said as he stumbled to his feet. "We needs to track down the scurvy lad."

Rocky scowled. "Blast it, Pip. I'm an engineer, not an inspector!"

"Be that as it may, sir," I said. "I have no intention of allowing my assailant to wander freely among the good passengers and crew people. Besides, he stole my purse."

I attempted to stand, but my knees were shaking. The whole confounded situation reminded me why I had wanted to resign from my post with the Society in the first place. Was it really a suitable profession for anyone, particularly a young woman who was still young enough to remarry if she put her mind to it?

Despite the man's nickname, Rocky was as soft a personality as the pirate. He reached his hand down and assisted me to stand. "Miss Knight, leave it to us. We'll find him."

"I do hope I'm included in that *we*," I said.

"Now, Miss Knight—"

"Don't *Miss Knight* me in that tone of voice, sir," I said. "I'm perfectly capable of handling myself despite being a woman. Besides, I believe I know who is responsible for my attacks."

Pip puffed out his chest again. "Point 'im out, miss. We ain't gonna let 'im get away again."

"I'm sure you won't."

"Is this your bag, miss?" Rocky asked and held up what was indeed my bag. "I found it back there in the intersection."

"It is! What an odd thief," I said.

But when Rocky lowered the bag into my hands, I realized it was no odd thief at all. Even so,

I reached into the purse and felt around, just in case I was mistaken. And I prayed I was.

I pulled my purse open widely and frantically searched the contents a second and third time.

"You missin' somethin', miss?" Pip asked.

I closed my eyes and leaned against the wall. I wasn't the fainting type, but I was suddenly feeling quite woozy.

"Indeed, I am. It seems my attacker is also a very particular thief."

Pip was right. This had been a trap, and now an agent of unknown motivation possessed the pyramid.

Chapter Nineteen

I wasn't sure what disturbed Prof. Runal more: the disappearance of the pyramid, or the presence of two humans who now had to be included in our conversation.

"How do we know it's not these two who set you up?" Prof. Runal asked at the finale of my recitation of the evening's events. He jerked his chin toward our two companions.

"I'm sure it's not, sir," I said.

We were in the chief engineer's quarters, which were larger than mine but slightly smaller than the captain's. It was the largest room we could access which could offer us a certain degree of privacy.

Prof. Runal sat in the only chair available,

glancing between the pirate and the chief engineer. "Are you quite sure about that?"

Pip's face looked like a storm cloud had met a craggy cliff. But he held his tongue and contented himself with a dark glower.

Rocky's expression soured, and he hadn't been happy to begin with. "Oi, I'm quite sure. I'm an engineer, not a thief. And as for Pip, I vouch for him. He's the most honest man I've yet to find."

Prof. Runal huffed a laugh. "If you say so. Very well. We shall go on the assumption that these two are innocent of the crime."

Pip grunted.

"It's now more urgent than ever that we find the culprit, Miss Knight," the professor continued. "In just over a week, we will be in the Suez Canal, at which point our thief can alight with relative ease and disappear into the crowds. We'll lose the pyramid forever."

The chief engineer and the pirate glanced at each other knowingly.

"What is it, then?" Prof. Runal asked. "Out with it! I can see you're up to something."

"See here, sir," Rocky said. He rested a booted foot on his bed and leaned an elbow on the knee. "It's not us who're up to something.

We had our suspicions before, about a certain pair."

Pip nodded. "You tell 'im, chief."

"I intend to. This here couple, well, I've seen them on this route on more than one occasion. They claim to be siblings, but I have my doubts. They look nothing alike, and they're always traveling together. They don't always use the S.S. *Suez*. I believe they try out different ships in order to disguise their activities, but chief engineers chat amongst themselves. You know how it is, sir."

"Indeed. Indeed, I do," the professor agreed and gestured for Rocky to continue.

"Well, then. The lady is quite remarkable in her appearance. She certainly doesn't blend in with the general population, even among the first-class passengers."

I allowed myself a moment of self-congratulatory pride. "I had suspected her all along. She's at the top of my list."

"See, chief," Pip said in his gravelly voice. "The miss, she's a smart one."

"Indeed, she is," Prof. Runal said. "You are no doubt referring to Lady Larrona and Lord Voleur. Of what crime do you accuse them?"

"Sir, you are aware of the trade in antiquities."

The professor nodded, his face uncharacteristically serious. "I am, sir. A nefarious trade, indeed. Robbing the Empire of its most precious historical relics."

"Then you've also heard of a recent string of museum thefts?"

"I have."

Rocky pushed away from his bed. "We suspect this couple is deeply involved in both the thefts and the resulting sale of ancient artifacts. I won't go into all the reasoning, but we need to be keeping an eye on them."

"Artifacts?" I repeated and turned to the professor. "Lady Larrona caught me on the deck while I was attempting to solve the puzzle."

"What puzzle?" Prof. Runal asked. "This is no time for children's games, Beatrice."

"The pyramid, sir. It's actually a puzzle. Remember you said it was the key? I initially assumed you meant the pyramid itself was the key."

"And now?"

"I believe if you solve the puzzle, it opens up to give you an actual key."

"Remarkable," the professor boomed. "Fantastical. Continue, Miss Knight."

"I was on deck, tucked behind one of the life rafts. It was in a location that passengers wouldn't naturally enter. So I was quite surprised when she made an appearance so abruptly by my side. I hid the pyramid, but it's possible she caught a glimpse of it. In which case, her interest would have been piqued, possibly enough that she made a second attempt against me."

The professor nodded. "But why would she have suspected you in the first place and attempted to enter your cabin that first night?"

For that, I had no answer. But Rocky did.

"She must've observed what we did, sir. With all due respect, neither Pip nor I believed that this young lass was your niece. There's very little family resemblance."

Pip nodded. "True. She's fair and pretty. He ain't nothin' of that."

The professor grumbled under his breath but refused to comment.

I covered my smile with a cough, then nodded at Prof. Runal's questioning gaze.

The professor clapped his hands once. "You're quite right, my good sir. Miss Knight is in fact my employee. All aboveboard and legitimate, I assure you. The little piece of antiquities that Lady

Larrona probably stole is critical to the survival of the British Empire's interests in North Africa."

Silence descended, although it could never be truly silent on a ship at sea. The ocean's condition was progressively worsening, and it took out its irritation on the S.S. *Suez*. Waves slapped heavily against the hull and tossed the ship to and fro. The walls creaked and groaned while the captain and crew battled the ever-larger waves. Rain slashed against the porthole, while the distant rumble of the engine could still be heard echoing through the floors. Even the piping seemed to resonate with all of the noises, magnifying them.

"Well, Miss Knight," Prof. Runal said and slapped his large hands on his thighs. "There's nothing for it, then."

I sighed. "I fear you're correct, sir."

Rocky straightened and blocked our exit. "What's this?"

"Perhaps it's best you not know," the professor said and stood.

The chief engineer leaned against his door. "See here. I know I'm only the chief engineer, but I'm one of the senior staff and report directly to the captain. I can't be having all of this nonsense happening under my watch. Now out with it."

"We need to retrieve that artifact," Prof. Runal said.

"And at the same time," I added, "perhaps we can help you resolve your mystery."

Rocky narrowed his eyes, but Pip grinned. It was a frightening sight.

"You gonna bust into them cabins, ain't you?" the pirate asked.

Rocky grumbled, "Blast it all, I'm an engineer, not a common thief."

I patted his arm. "Don't worry, sir. We'll make sure you're a very uncommon thief."

Chapter Twenty

It was always easier breaking into a place when you were escorted by a pirate and an engineer.

At least, that was my assumption as we four stood outside Lady Larrona's cabin. I turned expectantly to Chief Engineer Rocky, and he to me.

"The keys, sir," Prof. Runal prompted.

"Only the captain and the chief steward have the master key for the cabins," Rocky admitted.

"I knew this was too easy," I said. "Can we ask Chief Steward Stewart to loan his?" I pulled out my lock pick set in anticipation of the negative response.

Pip shook his head and crossed his arms over his chest.

The engineer scoffed. "Him? He won't help us,

lass. He takes his job very seriously. Not that I disapprove, mind you. But it's to the point he'd rather see the ship sink than intrude on the rights and privileges of his first-class passengers."

"Then it's a jolly good thing we have no such inhibitions," Prof. Runal said, his voice booming around us. "None at all, as a matter of fact. Isn't that right, Miss Knight?"

"Indeed it is, sir," I said and put my lock picks to use.

Pip whistled appreciatively, and I couldn't help the flush of pleasure at the approval. The door swung open, and I stepped inside first, ignoring Rocky's hiss of warning.

As fashionable as Lady Larrona was in public, her cabin was a disaster zone.

"Goodness," I exclaimed. "Doesn't she know what the closet is for?" I stepped over a stack of clothes and around a pile of fashionable shoes.

"Perhaps she's using the closet for another purpose," Rocky said. "Maybe to hide a thing or two?"

"Hopefully not anybody's skeleton," I said and dodged around a hat that had so many feathers, it looked like it was about to come alive. I reached the other side of the room without disturbing the clutter and chaos, and opened the narrow closet. Pip whistled again, and Rocky hooted.

"Looks like we were right, lad," he said and thumped Pip on the back. "Maybe I should be an investigator. At this rate, the brig'll be a busy place."

The closet was crammed from top to bottom with carefully wrapped packages of unusual shapes and sizes. I only had to unwrap one of them for us to confirm Rocky and Pip's suspicions. I held up a vase, clearly of ancient origin.

"We gonna arrest 'em now?" Pip asked. "Or can we make 'em walk the plank? Please?"

"I see why you like him," the professor said under his breath to me.

"No plank-walking allowed," Rocky said with a certain degree of disappointment. "But we can certainly throw them into the brig without being too gentle about it, and keep them there until the authorities can collect them."

"Oh. Okay," Pip said.

He looked so crestfallen that I blurted out, "And I'm sure everyone will be happy to acknowledge your role in the arrest of the great museum thieves, Pip."

Rather than cheer him up, I only added to his

horror. "Oh, no, miss. Ain't no one can see me. If the pirates hear of it, they'll wanna catch hold o' me. I'm a disgrace to the ways of the open seas. I—"

"Poppycock," Prof. Runal said. "You may be a disaster of a pirate, but you're a very fine sailor indeed."

Pip frowned, as if he wasn't quite sure if this was a compliment or an insult.

I continued to unwrap packages and open boxes. "But we still have one problem, sir. It seems the pyramid isn't among the items here."

"That is wretched news, terrible indeed." The professor sighed. "It seems I shall have to resort to my backup plan, then."

"A backup plan, sir?"

"One must always have a backup plan, dear Beatrice. It's more essential than a lock pick set and tea leaves."

"I wouldn't go that far, but to which backup plan do you refer?" I asked, my stomach tightening as I thought of the possibilities.

"No need for you to worry about it, my dear. None at all." The professor marched out of the room, leaving Rocky, the pirate and myself staring at each other in amazement.

"I'm sure he won't cause too much trouble," I tried to reassure the chief engineer and myself.

"I should hope he causes no trouble at all," Rocky retorted.

I hesitated and nibbled at my lower lip. "To be honest, I cannot promise you that—"

"What!" a woman's shriek rudely interrupted me.

I jumped to my feet, clutching a ceramic statue that was probably older than the British Empire and stared at Lady Larrona's astonished expression.

Not only was she fashionable, but she was also quick in mind and on her feet. She spun around and raced down the corridor before we could react to her presence.

"Now where do you think you can go? We're on the ocean, m'lady!" Chief Engineer Rocky shouted before bustling after her.

"Maybe she's gonna jump the ship," Pip said before trotting after Rocky. "Wait for me. I wanna see!"

"I'll keep looking through the loot," I called after them. Chasing after villains once the mystery was solved was dreadfully anticlimactic.

A thorough search of the cabin resulted in a great many pieces of valuable art and antiquities, but no small pyramid. By the time I had repackaged all the items, the captain appeared, his bearded face redder than I remembered it.

"Who would've guessed?" Captain McCormick huffed as he stared at the narrow bed which was covered in wrapped-up valuables. "A master thief, on my ship."

"Did they catch her?"

"They did, and her accomplice, that rascal Lord Voleur. All thanks to you, Miss Knight. I should've suspected something. He won far too many of our card games. Probably cheated."

I decided not to repeat the professor's comment regarding the captain's complete inability to win a card game even if Lady Luck sat on his head. Instead, I murmured some polite words, briefly described the artifacts recovered and left him to his work.

Disappointed at the loss of the pyramid but buoyed by the successful arrest of the museum thieves, I wandered the deck in search of Prof. Runal. It was late in the evening, the sky dark with storm clouds that had yet to make good on their threatening appearance. A cool, gusty wind nipped at my face and hands.

A few other passengers were taking an after-dinner constitutional, and we nodded at each other as I passed them. Mrs. Spratt suggested I stroll with her and Mr. Spratt, but I mumbled an excuse and continued on my way.

I was about to return to my cabin after failing to find the professor when I heard an aggressive shout, followed by a kerfuffle. It sounded like two men wrestling with an enraged bull. I was fairly certain the S.S. *Suez* didn't have any livestock onboard, but I could only pray it did.

"You're under arrest for sabotage, sir!" one of the men yelled.

"Oh, bother," I said.

Hoping I was wrong but dreading that I wasn't, I ran in the direction of the noise. Pip and Rocky appeared around the side of a life raft. Between them was a slightly disheveled but defiant Prof. Runal.

I skidded to a stop in front of them. "What is the meaning of this?"

"Apologies, Miss Knight," Rocky said.

I glanced at Pip, who refused to meet my gaze.

"Don't apologize to me, sir," I said. "Apologize to the professor, and unhand him at once."

Rocky shook his head, a stubborn expression settling into his features. "I fear not, lass. For we caught him in the act. No sooner had we escorted Lady Larrona and Lord Voleur into the brig, then we found your employer engaging in acts of sabotage."

I glowered at the three of them, tempted to put my walking stick to use. Men were such ego-driven and emotional creatures, including the werewolf kind. "Professor Runal would never … Or rather, what sabotage?"

"Sabotage?" a woman gasped.

I spun around. Mrs. Spratt and her scrawny husband stood nearby, gawking at the scene.

"Move along, Mrs. Spratt," I said. "There's nothing for you to see here."

"I should hope not," the woman said and hauled her husband away from us as if criminal intent was a contagious disease. "One thinks one is secure from undesirable elements when one purchases a first-class ticket, but it seems they allow anyone entrance nowadays."

I waited for the Spratt couple to disappear around the corner before repeating my question.

The professor cleared his throat. Without a hint of remorse, he said, "I did what I had to do, Beatrice. Only the most logical course of action."

"Which was—"

"We can't risk our thief escaping from the ship."

"How would one escape when there are miles of ocean surrounding us?"

"Never underestimate the desperate."

"And how did you intend to keep the thief on the ship?" I asked even though I suspected the response.

"Why, the answer is obvious, Beatrice, my dear. I sabotaged all of the life rafts, of course. They're completely un-seaworthy. Now we have our thief trapped!"

As if punctuating the professor's sentence, a loud wave of thunder crashed overhead, followed by a crack of lightning.

Chapter Twenty-One

"What were you thinking?" I demanded as I paced in front of the bars between me and the professor.

Across the room, another set of bars separated me from the museum thieves. Lady Larrona gripped the bars and shook them, as if by sheer force of will she could rip them away.

"Just you wait until I get out of here, young woman," she hissed. "No one does this to me. No one! Do you hear me?"

I waved a hand dismissively in her direction. "You're the least of our concerns, Lady Larrona. As for your threats, they are neither terrifying nor meaningful. I've faced beasts far more fierce than you. Speaking of which." I faced the professor.

"What do you have to say for yourself? Be quick. Pip is waiting for me outside."

The professor was stretched out on a narrow, metal bed. He seemed as comfortable as if he were in his own cabin rather than in the ship's prison. "Nothing beyond what I've already explained, my dear, nothing at all. We can't have that pyramid leaving in another person's luggage. You must find the culprit, whatever it takes."

He rolled onto his side and propped his head up with an arm. The bed squeaked in protest. "Do you hear me, Beatrice? At all costs."

The ship tilted slightly to one side, then to another as waves buffeted it with ever-increasing force.

"The cost might be very high indeed," I said. "With the life rafts now inoperable, what shall we do if the storm becomes too ferocious for the ship to handle?"

The professor smiled. "My dear Beatrice, if this ship is sunk by the storm, I assure you those life rafts are of little use to us. We'll drown either way."

"Still, I can't believe you sabotaged the life rafts. Oh, actually, wait. Of course I can believe it! It's something you would do." I resumed my pacing and ignored our audience. "And this is exactly why I wanted to resign. It's why I …"

I bit off my sentence before I could say more. But my hand instinctively slipped into my jacket pocket and wrapped around the small tin box.

"It's why you're taking those pills?" the professor asked, his voice soft and without judgment.

I glanced up and stared into his eyes. They were dark brown, compassionate and too intelligent for my own good. There was no point in arguing. He'd discovered my secret.

"But how—"

He tapped the side of his nose. "A werewolf's nose always knows."

"A pox on you and your kind."

"There's still time to stop, you know. Just throw them out. You're not an addict, Beatrice. Not yet. But you will be if you continue."

"That's the idea."

"You're better than that." He sighed. "I fear I might have failed you. I underestimated the impact of …" He hesitated. "Of recent events. For that, I am deeply sorry."

I was unable to respond for a moment as something seemed to grab hold of my throat and clench tightly. When I finally dared speak, I said, "I think I prefer you in here."

"Toss them into the sea. I promise when we return to London, I shall find the best help for you. We'll work through this together."

I leaned close to the bars and hissed, "The *best* help? I don't want a vampire wiping my memories, thank you very much."

He blinked a few times, as if trying to adjust to a change in lighting. "But my dear Miss Knight, some memories really aren't worth keeping."

"I give up. You're truly incorrigible. And our prime suspects are already locked away, their cabins searched from top to bottom. So where should I go now?"

"What do you mean, your *prime* suspects?" Lord Voleur demanded and kicked at one of the bars, then muttered a curse at the resulting pain.

"We're having a private conversation here," I said and glared at the man. "Do you mind?"

"Beatrice, I have full faith in your ability to solve this puzzle," Prof. Runal said. "As you can see, I'm incapacitated at the moment."

I held up my walking stick. "I could open that lock for you in a jiffy."

"It's best we don't attract more attention to ourselves than we already have."

"Open our locks instead," Lord Voleur said and shook the bars. "We'll pay you handsomely."

I frowned over my shoulder. "The only thing handsome about you is that you are now where you belong, behind bars."

Ignoring Lord Voleur's curses and Lady Larrona's threats, I marched out of the brig and into the corridor where Pip was waiting for me.

"It seems I'm on my own," I said to Pip.

I didn't mean to make it sound like a complaint or an admission of weakness, but my tone had a dejected air even to my ears.

Pip patted my back, almost knocking me to my knees. "Don't you worry, miss. You ain't alone. I ain't goin' anywheres."

"That is quite literally true," I said. "None of us are going anywhere off this ship until we reach the canal. I think it's time I paid a visit to our three guests who have remained in their cabins despite meals, card games and storms."

Pip frowned. "You mean the privacy cabins?"

"Exactly. It's one thing to need a bit of alone time. But to spend two weeks in voluntary isolation seems a bit of a stretch, don't you think?"

Pip shrugged. "You's the one who's the thinker, miss. Will you be needin' me help?"

I tried to imagine standing in front of one of the cabin doors with the hulking, scarred-face pirate looming behind me.

"Not this time, Pip. But I will certainly reach out to you if I need your assistance."

On that agreeable note, we went our separate ways. He returned to the bowels of the ship and the engine room, and I went to the first-class quarters. I roamed the passageways until I reached the door of the first mystery guest, Mrs. Twitcher.

I straightened up and lifted my chin. At my height, I couldn't afford to slouch. I focused on looking sweet and innocent while promising myself that resignation from the Society was still an option, particularly if my employer remained in the brig for long enough, or if the ship sank in a storm. Then I rapped sharply on the cabin door.

Steps shuffled toward me. "I didn't order room service." The frail voice was scratchy and tight, as if the woman had recently strained her voice.

As I was never too impressed with the pretense of feminine weakness, I paid no heed to the first impression the voice provided. The person on the other side of the door might sound like a little old woman with weak limbs, but she could just as easily be a monster in disguise.

"Mrs. Twitcher, I do apologize for the intrusion. I'm Miss Knight, a fellow passenger. And I'm in need of a moment of your time, if you please."

"But I requested full privacy. Only room service is allowed. Are you here for room service?"

"No, but—"

"Then go away."

"It's a matter of urgency."

The sigh that crept through the cracks around the door was one of an aggrieved and exhausted person. "Very well. But only a moment."

The door creaked open just a crack, and a pair of bulbous eyes blinked up at me.

"Mrs. Twitcher?" I asked.

The door opened a bit farther, and I had a full view of one of the mystery guests. As her voice suggested, she was a tiny woman and barely reached my chest, and I was by no means tall. Her white hair was pulled back into a tight bun, and her eyes were so pale that I wondered if she was perhaps blind. Her back was hunched over, and she had to tilt her head to the side to meet my gaze.

"Yes. What is it?"

I didn't have to squint to see the truth. Mrs.

Twitcher was as frail and as human as she looked. Chances were slim that this was the pyramid thief. But I couldn't very well leave now that I had intruded on her privacy.

I forced a smile. "I wanted to check up on you. To ensure that you're comfortable and have the companionship you need."

She opened the door fully, revealing a room more chaotic than Lady Larrona's. "As comfortable as one can be on a tub floating in the middle of the ocean, and I have no need for companionship, thank you for asking. But since you're already here, won't you come in?"

I gulped, but felt I had no choice except to comply with the invitation. As I did, I tried not to stare at the numerous birds perched on every surface. One of them — a bright green parrot — squawked and flew at me. I instinctively ducked, and the beast landed on my head where it flapped its wings, smacking my ears.

"Oh, Charlie, try not to poop on the nice lady's head," Mrs. Twitcher said as she closed the door and locked me in her cabin. "He's full of mischief, that one, but he's really a lovable fellow. Do you like birds?"

I became acutely aware of the dozens of avian

eyes watching me as I tried to find a place I could sit that wasn't covered in some element of bird. "I can't say I don't like them," I finally said, opting for a tactful version of truthfulness.

"They're marvelous, aren't they? Far superior to human companions, I can tell you. Not many people appreciate them as you and I do."

I blinked rapidly. I wasn't sure how she thought my statement indicated any level of approval, but I left her to her assumptions and attempted to extract Charlie's claws from my hair.

"How are the other passengers?" Mrs. Twitcher asked as she sat on a chair covered in feathers, dandruff and possibly bird excrement.

I gave up on searching for a clean seat. I remained standing in the middle of her cabin, a parrot squawking on my head while a pair of colorful lovebirds fluttered around me. "They're well enough, I suppose. As far as humans go, that is. None are as interesting as you, Mrs. Twitcher."

She tittered. "Us avian lovers are our own breed of people, are we not?"

"You are indeed. Well, it's been a pleasure—"

"But you haven't met Sir Lancelot yet." She sat up, startling the lovebirds into flapping against my face.

"Sir Lancelot?"

"He was my first."

I waved the lovebirds away, coughed feathers out of my mouth and managed to remove Charlie, who glided onto the bed.

A colorful macaw croaked, "Pretty bird, who's a pretty bird."

"Yes, you are, my darling," Mrs. Twitcher cooed as she hobbled toward the narrow closet.

I was starting to dislike those closets very much.

She opened it and reached inside with both hands. When she stepped away, she held out before her an object that almost caused me to shriek before I swallowed it with a small hiccup.

"Isn't he magnificent?" Mrs. Twitcher held out the stuffed gray parrot as if it were a trophy she was bestowing upon me.

I stared at Sir Lancelot. The bright yellow glass eyes glittered back at me. I supposed the thing had once been a handsome bird when it had been alive a few decades ago. But at this stage, most of its feathers had either fallen off or had been partially devoured by age or mites.

"He's definitely original." I took a step backward and felt for the doorknob.

"He is, isn't he? Do you want to stroke him?

He's so lovable." Mrs. Twitcher lifted up a gnarled, shaking hand and rubbed the head of the stuffed bird. A tuft of small feathers floated around her as she did so.

"I'm good, thank you," I said. "And on that note … Would you look at the time? How it flies when one is having a fit … I mean, fun. I bid you good evening, Mrs. Twitcher."

Before Mrs. Twitcher could thrust her stuffed pet at me, I twirled around, yanked open the door and ran.

Chapter Twenty-Two

I decided to call it quits for the night. I was used to eventful evenings, but this had been unusually so. Dinner, an attack, the discovery and consequent arrests of two antiquities thieves, followed by the arrest of my employer and the chat with the bird-obsessed Mrs. Twitcher had left me feeling almost faint.

And I'd accomplished all that without the benefit of even one morsel of the dessert.

I sighed and collapsed onto my bed. "I wonder if I can order room service," I said right before I fell asleep and into a nightmare.

"I shall find you, little girl. I shall find you and make you suffer as I have," Koki's voice chased me through my dreams.

I escaped Koki but found myself back in my marital home, standing over the body of my husband.

"He's quite dead, I'm afraid to say," the professor murmured softly. "I'm sorry, Beatrice, but he is very much deceased."

"There is nowhere you can run," Koki shrieked, her voice echoing in the room. "There is nowhere you can hide where I won't find you. I'm coming!"

I gasped and jerked awake as the ship lurched from side to side like an old train on a rickety set of rails.

"It's okay, Beatrice," Gideon whispered.

I blinked at the faintly luminescent outline of my ghost husband. "Of course it's okay. Why wouldn't it be?"

He pretended to sit at the edge of my bed, almost close enough for me to touch if he'd had a body to touch. "You were crying. Screaming for help. You still have those nightmares, don't you?"

I rubbed my face and looked toward the port-hole. The window showed only darkness. "It's nothing, Gideon."

"Shall I sing you to sleep like I used to?"

I collapsed against my pillow and gazed up at him. I was still fully dressed, not having had the energy to change into my nightclothes. That was what happened when one didn't indulge in a bit of dessert after dinner.

"You don't have to do that," I said while praying he would ignore my false protests and sing.

He smiled, not in a mischievous, naughty way but the soft, warm smile of love. "Close your eyes."

I did so, and his soft voice wrapped around me, the words a familiar lullaby.

"It won't work, you know," I murmured just before I fell into the deepest sleep I'd had since Gideon's demise.

The next time I opened my eyes, the watery light of a rainy day filled my cabin, and I felt as rested as if I were back at home with Gideon.

I prepared myself for a busy day. I was energized and determined to find the pyramid and hopefully free my employer. At the very least, I needed to give him a final decision regarding my resignation, whatever that decision might be.

I still wasn't convinced I should remain with the Society. If this was the sort of adventures my continued employment would provide me, it might be safer to be unemployed and dependent. Then again, dependency on my aunt and uncle was even less desirable than tromping about a ship, chasing after a thief.

Breakfast was a quiet affair. I couldn't help but notice the sly looks cast in my direction. Soft whispers followed me, and the waitstaff were very quick to bring me my dishes before scuttling away.

Only Chief Officer Frenchy met my gaze and nodded formally at me. "Bonjour, mademoiselle. You had a good evening last night?"

"As much as one can hope for," I said.

"Ze stories of your adventures have made ze rounds," he said and smirked.

I could tell that the stories had spread beyond the crew. Mrs. Spratt was sitting at a new table and was whispering to another couple with unconcealed zeal while casting obvious glances in my direction. By lunchtime, all the first-class passengers would hear the story of my employer's disgraced condition, and none would give me the time of day.

That suited me well enough. I'd already questioned all of them and found them unworthy to make my list of suspects. And now that Lady Larrona and Lord Voleur were similarly crossed off, I was left more puzzled than ever before. There was nothing for it but to knock on the door of the second mystery guest. I only prayed her cabin wasn't full of birds, alive or otherwise.

Immediately after breakfast, I beat a hasty retreat from the dining room and entered the living quarters of the first-class passengers. I checked my list. Mrs. Twitcher was now crossed off, being guilty only of mild insanity and a parrot obsession. That left cabins eight and twenty-seven. The first was occupied by Miss Devin, who had finished a sizable breakfast, as evidenced by a number of empty dishes left outside her door, waiting to be cleared.

I knocked. "Miss Devin?"

"Who cares to know?" a shockingly deep yet vaguely feminine voice demanded.

"Miss Knight, one of your fellow passengers. Do you have a moment—"

The occupant wrenched open the door, and a giant of a woman loomed over me.

I stumbled backward in case she was about to strike me. "Miss Devin?"

She glanced down the corridor, then in the other direction. "Are you quite alone?"

That was a treacherous question. For if I admitted to being alone, what foul action would she commit against my person? And yet, her deep frown suggested she was worried and perhaps wouldn't respond to me if I claimed to be with another.

"My companion is currently indisposed," I said, deciding on a middle ground.

"Is he dead?" She fixed me with a look that startled me even more than her giant appearance. One of her eyes was a light gray, the other dark brown, almost black.

"That depends on which one," I said, her appearance startling the truth out of me.

"Yes. I suspected as much. Come in quickly, before they follow you."

I gripped my walking stick and entered her cabin. At the very least, there were no birds flapping around. Instead, crystals hung from every handle and light fitting. One had been nailed so that it hung in front of the round window, casting pale little rainbows as it twirled with the movement of the ship. A crystal ball rested on the pillow of the bed. Several incense sticks burned from a clay pot filled with soil. A sharp, cloying perfume wafted from the sticks.

"Check again," Miss Devin said. "Did he follow you?"

I stared up at Miss Devin. Despite her size, she seemed vulnerable. Her strangely colored eyes were framed by thick eyelashes, emphasizing the fear in their depths. I suspected if she wasn't so suspicious, she would have a pretty smile.

"I don't think he did."

"One never knows with the dead," Miss Devin said and waved me over.

"You see them, then?" I squinted at her and caught a strong tremor in her energy. She was human but gifted with the sight. Most people who professed to be psychics really weren't, but she was legitimately talented.

"I do. I see them everywhere," she intoned. "They're nuisances, to be honest."

"I quite concur," I said, feeling sympathy and camaraderie with the woman. "I can barely move along London's streets without walking through one."

"Exactly. I'd hoped that being on the ship would give me a break from them. But your ghost has moved into my closet." She tilted her head in the direction of the narrow closet in the far corner.

I glared at it. "I've decided I really don't like ship closets."

"A wise decision. They're too small to be of any use for storing women's fashions, but they're perfectly sized for a ghost."

"Not to mention stuffed parrots and stolen artifacts."

"Scandalous. Do you want to see the rascal?" She gestured to the narrow closet.

"Not particularly."

"He's a dastardly fellow, full of mischief. I can see it in his eyes."

"Yes, that sounds about right. Do you want me to take him with me?"

"I would be most obliged, Miss Knight."

I exhaled heavily and strode toward the closet. "Gideon, come out at once."

Nothing.

"Gideon, I hereby give you permission to float through solid surfaces. And I shan't lecture you on the lack of manners entailed by that action."

Still, there was no sign of the ghost.

"Really, Gideon. You do vex me." I reached out and yanked open the closet door, then tripped back. "Good heavens, you're not Gideon."

A peg-legged, one-eyed ghost squinted at me. "Who's Gideon?"

"My dead husband. Who are you?"

The potbellied ghost puffed out his broad chest. "I'm what you call a pirate hunter. And I've been on the search for the scurvy dog who knifed me in the back, then ran off with my gold. You wouldn't happen to know of any pirates on the ship, now would you, lassie?"

I was grateful he only had one eye with which to stare at me. The other was covered by a black patch. "Truth be told, you look rather like a pirate yourself."

He scowled. "Is it because of the leg, then? Or the eyepatch? Those are such stereotypes, you know."

"Indeed, sir. I am aware of stereotypes. And my deepest apologies for using one against you."

"Although I will admit I once had a parrot. A beautiful, big, gray parrot. A vicious woman stole him from me. You wouldn't happen to have seen her, now would you?"

"Does she have a name, by any chance?"

"Aye, she does. Mrs. Twitcher. My wife and a thief."

"Oh." I glanced at Miss Devin, who shrugged.

Mr. Twitcher hopped out of the closet, shuddered and scrambled back in. "If you see her or my parrot, you let me know, won't you?"

"I shall keep an eye out for her. Maybe even two," I said and closed the door. "Gracious."

I turned to Miss Devin. "You wouldn't happen

to know anything about a lost artifact?" I asked and glanced hopefully at her crystal ball. "It's rather important, and someone has recently stolen it."

Miss Devin's wide shoulders slumped. "The ball's not working anymore. The moment the ship left port, my sight failed me in all things except one. I can still see ghosts."

"Such a shame."

"It's outrageous, actually. I hope you find what you're looking for. And do come around to visit me again. I requested privacy because people are rather startled by my looks. But it would be nice to chat with someone who understands these things." She waved at the closet.

After promising her I would pay her a visit in due course, I bid her good day and stood in the hallway, wondering what to do next. I pulled out my notebook and crossed Miss Devin off the list.

There was only one suspect remaining: the occupant of room twenty-seven. I set off down the corridor, hoping I could finish the interview in time for midmorning tea, then changed my mind. If the previous two cabins were anything to go by, I was going to need a recharge first.

Chapter Twenty-Three

After the interview with Miss Devin and Mr. Twitcher, I retired to the dining room for refreshments and fresher air. I was the only passenger. Chief Steward Stewart was lording over the waiting staff, directing their setup for the tea service in minuscule detail.

"You fool," he exclaimed and threatened to cuff a young man against his ear. "The distance between the cutlery and the plate should be exactly one inch. No more, no less. Does this look like an inch to you? No, it does not! This is unacceptably sloppy!"

I recognized the young man as Jack Clark or Eleanor. She mumbled apologies, shifted the cutlery a hair's breadth to meet the exacting standards of the chief steward, then hurried over to where I sat at my usual table.

"Have you been promoted?" I asked as she took my order.

"Unfortunately, yes, but just for a day or two," she whispered. "I'm substituting for one of the servers who had an attack of the nerves."

"I can't imagine why," I said.

Eleanor giggled. "Crew prefer climbing the riggings to setting the tables."

"Gracious. The dining room sounds like a demotion, not a promotion."

Eleanor's hands shook as she fiddled with the spacing of the cutlery on my table. "He's going to see through me, for certain. What shall I do?"

"You can always pretend to have an attack of the nerves, as well. With him as your overlord, nobody would be surprised in the least."

"But then the ship's doctor will have to inspect me, and I can't afford that, either."

I sympathized with her dilemma. "You'll manage. Keep your head down and—"

"Sailor Clark!" Chief Steward Stewart shouted across the room. "Stop your dawdling. Take the order, and hurry up about it!"

I winced. "A cup of Earl Gray, if you don't mind."

She almost curtsied as she backed away, then caught herself just in time. Instead, she gave a slight bow, turned around and practically ran out of the room toward the kitchen.

A few moments later, the waiting staff had finished setting up for midmorning tea and disappeared before the chief steward found some other means with which to torment them. I enjoyed a few brief minutes of solitude before other passengers began to enter.

"Quite a brisk morning," Mrs. Spratt said as she bullied her husband toward their table. "And the waves! It looks like that storm is finally about to arrive. Mark my words, Mr. Spratt. We shall be in the middle of a serious storm."

"So it seems," I said as they sat at a table close to mine. "Perhaps it would be better if you remained below deck."

Mrs. Spratt sniffed and stared pointedly at the empty chair normally occupied by Prof. Runal. "And what of your companion? How does he fair?"

"Well enough. His new accommodations are remarkably comfortable. Let's just hope we won't need to use the life rafts."

"Whatever do you mean by that?" Mrs. Spratt demanded and squeezed a teaspoon into submission.

"Can you imagine sitting in one of those small dinghies in the midst of a mighty storm that's strong enough to sink this ship?"

She gasped and placed a hand over her heart. "You are a most peculiar young lady, Miss Knight. Come on, Mr. Spratt. We shall sit elsewhere."

"That's a wise idea, given that peculiar tendencies are highly infectious," I said.

Mrs. Spratt huffed and puffed, but I achieved the desired results. The tables closest to me were now empty, and my privacy secured.

I pulled out the copy of the passenger manifest and glanced through the results. Most of the passengers and crew in first class had been interviewed or eliminated for one reason or another. There were only two possibilities remaining: the mysterious, privacy-requesting passenger in the third cabin, and the passengers in steerage. And despite Prof. Runal's reassurances that no one from steerage could ever possibly rise up to the first-class level, I still had my doubts.

Or what if Lady Larrona and Lord Voleur had hidden the pyramid somewhere else?

"Unlikely," I muttered as I tapped my pen against the paper. "Not when their closets still had space for other artifacts. They certainly weren't making an effort to hide those beyond putting them in their rooms. No. It's either the third private passenger, or steerage."

My mind made up, I finished my tea, staring out the window at the ever-darkening sky. It looked like nightfall rather than morning. Mrs. Spratt was correct. We were in for another storm, and this one looked more ferocious than the previous evening's rain.

"Holiday in the sun, he said. Ha. So much for that."

I slipped my notebook into my bag and looked up at Eleanor. Her face was flushed, her manner agitated, so I decided that perhaps the chief steward needed an excuse to visit the doctor.

As Chief Steward Stewart hurried past my table, shouting orders at the miserable and unfortunate Eleanor, I angled my walking stick in such a way as to interrupt his path. He tripped and staggered against the nearest occupied table, which — I was most satisfied to see — belonged to no other than Mrs. Spratt and her scrawny husband.

The good lady shrieked as the table rocked

under the weight of the chief steward. Her cup flew upward, its contents raining down on her. This caused her to tip backward to avoid the spray until gravity defeated her chair's efforts to stay upright. She and her seat rolled into the pathway of the assistant steward, who toppled over and collapsed onto the Spratt table. The table, which was already in a precarious situation, fell over. A small tidal wave of tea and crumpets splashed across the floor.

While the chief steward, assistant steward and Mrs. Spratt scrambled over each other and the destroyed tea service, Mr. Spratt remained untouched and unfazed in his chair. Indeed, the man had been astute enough to pick up his cup and saucer before the table had fallen over. He remained seated, sipping at his tea, a small smile playing on his lips.

"Help me, Mr. Spratt," his wife yelped as she attempted to stand on the now slippery patch of floor.

"You fool," Chief Steward Stewart yelled at the assistant steward.

Meanwhile, I set my cup down with great care, stood and glided past the mess, nodding discreetly at Eleanor on my way out.

After that highly satisfactory teatime experience,

I felt thoroughly revitalized and capable of approaching the third mystery passenger. As most of the first-class passengers were either in the dining room or huddled in their cabins recovering from sea-related ailments, the passageways were clear of all interference.

I approached cabin twenty-seven and rapped my knuckles sharply against the door. There was no response.

I pressed my ear against the surface and listened for any indication of movement or breath. Inhaling deeply, I caught only a whiff of women's perfume — proving that Prof. Runal was correct in his assumption — and a cat.

I glanced around, expecting Cairo to wrap around my ankles at any moment. But the corridor was empty, as was the cabin before me.

"But that's not possible," I said. "I certainly didn't see this passenger in the dining room."

There was nothing for it but to break into yet another cabin. It was rapidly becoming a habit. I removed my lock pick set and made quick work of opening the door.

"I shall have to inform the captain of the necessity of improving their locks," I whispered as I returned the set of tools to its small compartment in my walking stick and slid inside the room, closing the door behind me.

As I'd deduced, the cabin was empty of human life. All that remained was the delicate aroma of a woman's perfume and the musky scent of a cat. Given how Cairo moved around the ship with such ease, it didn't surprise me that the smart little feline had found its way into a cabin. It was a rather endearing creature, and it seemed the passenger had enjoyed having it with her.

But there was something wrong.

It took me a moment to identify the issue. In case I was mistaken, I checked under the bed and dared to open the closet door.

"What sort of a woman travels without any luggage?" I asked.

"A very clever one, I would say."

I didn't jump or squeak with surprise when Gideon materialized inside the narrow closet and winked at me.

"Gideon, by now you are quite aware of how I feel about your behavior." I waved a hand to gesture to his entire being. "Such disregard for another person's nerves is unacceptable."

He smirked. "Since when are you the type of woman to suffer bouts of bad nerves?"

"A valid question, and it's beside the point. If you wish to accompany me on my mission, then I must insist you behave like a living man."

He wagged his eyebrows in a suggestive manner. "It would be my pleasure."

"Good heavens," I huffed and turned away as he laughed at my discomfort.

I did a more thorough search of the cabin, which only confirmed my original observation. The occupant of number twenty-seven had brought no luggage with her, not even a toothbrush. In fact, the only proof of occupancy I could find were a few short black hairs belonging to Cairo and one very long strand of equally black hair which had snagged in a corner of the closet door.

I stared at the long hair and the cat's fur in my hand. "Most peculiar. Where do you think she could be?"

"The lady or the cat?" Gideon asked as he strolled around the room.

"The lady, of course. Why should I care where the cat is? I'm sure it's doing what cats tend to do: stalking unfortunate little beasts and tearing off their limbs before eating them."

"Such a graphic imagination, Beatrice. I do approve."

I sniffed disdainfully. "While I don't require your approval, I thank you for the compliment. A vivid imagination is one of the most essential tools for a paranormal investigator. It's why most humans are not cut out for the business."

"Are you accusing yourself of being human?"

I ignored the jibe and sat on the bed. "I suppose there's nothing for it, then."

"What now?" Gideon asked.

I wrapped the hairs in a handkerchief. "I'm going to visit steerage."

"You can't be serious."

"I can be, when I put my mind to it. There are no more suspects to be found up here."

"And far too many in second class, I'm sure."

"Snobbery will get you nowhere, Gideon." I slipped the hairs into my pocket and stood. "That said, I hope to find at least one suspect below. And if I'm lucky, maybe even two."

Chapter Twenty-Four

If first-class quarters were heaven, and the noisy, oily engine room was hell, then steerage was purgatory.

Such were the directions of my thoughts as I descended several staircases to reach the second-class level. While first-class passengers each had their own private cabin, steerage passengers shared a large, open hall with three levels of bunk beds pressed along the walls. Some families slept together on the floor on thin, dingy mattresses that made my sensitive nose twitch.

Despite the crowded conditions and lack of privacy, the passengers looked comfortable enough. Many of them were gathered around a long table that ran most of the length of the vast room. Tea and snacks had been set out, which was highly reassuring. I'd rather not interview humans who were irritable from insufficient food and beverage. There are few creatures more ferocious.

I kept to the edge of the room, surreptitiously studying the various passengers. They were an interesting mix of cultures and ethnicities, and many had black hair, which didn't help me narrow down possible suspects. I detected a number of non-English languages being used. Each group kept to their own, and I stood out by virtue of being well dressed and unaccompanied.

By the time I was halfway down the length of the great hall, I felt a presence stalking me. I pretended not to notice and lengthened my stride ever so slightly. A group of children were playing with cars they'd made out of cartons and other scraps. I knelt carefully in the middle of their game and chatted with them while using the opportunity to look around.

Two thuggish-looking fellows stood several paces away. They were standing close, engaged in a whispered, energetic conversation. One of them glanced sideways at me, then sneered.

I started looking for another exit, but there wasn't any. The only way out was the one door through which I had entered. If I tried to return at this moment, I'd have to pass the two men. The other option was to continue on my present course and circle around the far end of the long table.

I continued my stroll, occasionally finding some reason to turn part of the way around. My unwanted entourage maintained the distance between us. But the fact they were following me and not pretending otherwise made me clutch my walking stick closer as I mentally prepared to battle my way back to the door.

Toward the back of the hall, two women and three adolescent girls were clustered around a pot of burning coals, over which they held another pot. One of the women cooked a stew over their makeshift stove. The second woman was younger, her face unlined with the passing of years. The three girls giggled and whispered.

Their chatter ceased as I stopped outside of their circle. The older woman — her silver-streaked dark hair almost completely covered by a scarf — glanced up, then down to the stew. The younger one watched me with a mixture of curiosity and suspicion.

I glanced over my shoulder. The two men were a lot closer than before.

"It smells delicious," I said slowly, raising my voice over the soft thud of the engine in the background.

The younger woman opened her mouth as if to reply, but the older woman hissed and muttered something that included the name Delilah.

"Delilah, is it?" I asked.

Delilah started arguing with the older woman in a language that sounded almost like Arabic but wasn't, their voices muted as they huddled together.

"I'm looking for a toy pyramid. Have you seen one?" I asked.

The women stopped talking and stared at me.

"You know. Like the ones in Giza." I stroked the air with my hands, as if outlining a small pyramid. "Do you understand?"

The three girls giggled, then hid behind Delilah, who I assumed was the mother.

I was about to give up on manners and squint in order to study the women when a heavy hand fell on my shoulder and spun me around. The two thugs loomed over me.

With a thick accent, one of them said, "Your bag. Now. No belong here."

I stepped back. "I'm a tad confused. My bag doesn't belong here? Or I don't?"

"You want to die?"

I surreptitiously maneuvered my walking stick in preparation and rambled as I plotted out the fastest route back to the door. "Is that a trick question or a rhetorical one? I never quite know how to answer it, particularly in these sorts of situations."

The other thug scowled. "You—"

"I very much doubt anyone would answer that question with, 'Yes, please. I'd love to die. Kill me now.' And yet, you'd be surprised at the number of villainous characters who've asked me just that very question. But in case that wasn't a rhetorical question, let me reassure you of a simple fact: I have no wish to die. I actually have a wish for a long life and a cup of tea. Would you care to join me?"

The old woman shouted something in the strange almost-Arabic language, clearly unimpressed with the situation. The thugs shouted back, then jumped toward me at the same time.

I didn't bother with a clever, conversational approach. No one in this group appeared to appreciate witty banter. Instead, I crouched and spun at the same time, wielding my walking stick in order to trip up their legs. One man fell heavily on his back while the other tripped over him but managed to regain his balance.

"It's been lovely chatting with you," I told the ladies, then leaped to one side and began running back down the length of the hall.

The two men yelled what I could only imagine were obscenities in a foreign language. A tribal language, perhaps?

As it was neither important nor relevant to my current situation, I set the linguistic curiosity to one side and focused on dashing and dodging around clusters of passengers. They all seemed intent on enjoying the spectacle of a first-class passenger being chased by two of their own.

I didn't bother crying out for help. It was clear no one had any intention of providing it. If the sight of a lone woman being chased by two men wasn't enough to elicit a compassionate heart, then wasting my breath on screaming wouldn't do it.

Fingers raked against the back of my jacket, and I dodged to one side before my pursuer could get a solid grip. The change in direction put me on a collision course with the long table. Lifting up my skirt almost to my knees and grateful I was wearing boots that covered my legs, I prepared to jump.

I leaped onto an empty chair and from there onto the narrow wooden table. A few of the passengers screamed, including a man into whose toast I stepped, but most cheered and laughed.

So much for discretion, I thought as I bounded onto a chair on the other side. It tilted backward, and I jumped off just before it crashed to the floor. One of the thugs followed my example but must have slipped on a plate of butter. I glanced back in time to see the result of his misstep. His arms pinwheeled in a failed effort to defy gravity, and his legs flew upward. The butter plate crashed to the ground and slid toward me. The second thug stayed on the other side of the table and kept pace with me.

The entrance was only several steps away now. But as fast as I was, the thugs were faster. I knew I wasn't going to reach the doorway before one or the other tackled me to the ground. And I had no intentions of scuffing my boots or tearing my skirt. So I took the course of action that any paranormal investigator would take.

I pulled a small blowgun out from my walking stick, twirled around, aimed and fired. Or to be more accurate, I exhaled sharply.

The small dart hit the man at the base of the neck in that delicate hollow which has no bone underneath it. The dart's sedative was fast-acting, and by the time his companion rounded the end of the long table, the first man had collapsed to his knees, already falling asleep.

I didn't have time to insert a second dart, so I pressed two of the nails on top of my walking stick's fist. A blade *snicked* out from the other end. The second man skidded to a halt and squatted next to his companion, then glared up at me. He muttered some words in that strange dialect, and I'm quite certain they were a curse or possibly a threat. Maybe both.

"He'll be fine in a jiffy," I reassured him and the growing crowd that was approaching us. Keeping my stick up like a sword, I backed toward the entrance and only dared turn my back to steerage when I was safely in the passageway, the door between us closed.

I ran down corridors and up staircases, and didn't stop until I arrived at the dining room in time for lunch. I was quite breathless, but at least I'd worked up an appetite and a couple of suspects.

Chapter Twenty-Five

Chief Engineer Rocky McIntyre must've taken pity on my lonely condition, for he invited me to lunch at the senior crew's table. The captain wasn't around, which wasn't that surprising. Apart from the first night, he hadn't been seen at mealtimes. The senior crew took it in turns to represent him.

"Are you quite well, Miss Knight?" Rocky asked as he passed the casserole to me.

I laid a hand just under my chin and felt for my pulse. My heart was still beating faster than normal, although who could blame it? It was still recovering from my close call with the two bandits and the race through the ship.

Were those men connected with the women? Perhaps they'd only intended to protect their family.

Then why had the old woman sounded angry when she spoke to them? And why did they chase me all the way back down the hall once I had left the women alone? Did any of them have the pyramid?

"As fit as a fiddle," I said. "What news of my dear uncle?"

Rocky snorted. "There's no need for pretense with me, lassie. I know very well he's not your uncle."

"Very well. What news of my employer?"

Another disbelieving snort, followed by a small glass of something that from the smell of it wasn't water. "Well enough, I suppose. We make sure he's fed, at least. I wouldn't worry about it. When we reach Cairo, we'll hand him over to the authorities, who'll immediately deport him and send him back with us. Unfortunately, you may have to abandon your plans to tour the country. Not that you'd want to. Things are a wee bit uptight over there."

"And here as well." I ignored Rocky's puzzled expression and continued. "And what will happen with the other two? The museum thieves?"

"Oi, them! They'll be staying in the brig until we return to London. We've already sent a message to the authorities there. I suspect they'll receive an enthusiastic welcome when we drop anchor." He chuckled at the kind of enthusiastic welcome the thieves were going to have.

"Delightful, I'm sure."

We continued to eat, and I was grateful for the lack of conversation. When I sit at a dining table, I prefer to focus on eating rather than talking. I can never understand how people think the two are compatible activities. It seemed Rocky shared my disinclination to simultaneously attempt conversing and eating. Only after we had finished with the main course did he turn to me.

"You haven't by any chance seen Cairo?"

"I must confess this is my first visit to Egypt."

He huffed a laugh. "I was referring to the wee kitty. The captain's been missing his new pet. I'm sure the little beastie has simply wandered off to some corner or other for privacy. Or maybe one of the passengers has taken a liking and is feeding it treats to keep it close. That sometimes happens."

"I can't say I've seen it. But I'll let you know if it shows up."

He grunted and waved one of the serving staff to come clear the table.

"Is there anyone staying in cabin twenty-seven?" I asked.

"I'd have to check the manifest, but I believe we're full."

"Have you seen the occupant?"

Rocky had already lost interest now that he'd finished with lunch. He scraped back his chair and stood. "Any passenger staying in twenty-seven has requested privacy. I do my best to avoid those ones in particular. You'd do well to do the same. Good day, Miss Knight."

I glanced around the room, wondering what to do next. It seemed I had exhausted all our suspects. And while the two would-be bandits and their lady friends were suspicious, I had to agree with the professor. It was unlikely they could've snuck into first class so easily, particularly since they would have stood out with their darker skin and their clothes, which were out of keeping with English fashion.

I had made a decision to visit the professor and consult with him when one of the serving staff approached my side and held out a platter. Hoping it was dessert, I glanced up and sighed in disappointment.

"An invitation for you, miss," the young man said.

"Goodness, this is becoming quite the habit. I'm

not sure it's one I want." I plucked off the card, opened it and smiled.

Join me for dessert. Miss Devin.

Finally, some mention of dessert! It was a most appropriate use of an invitation card. As I had nothing else to do, and as the investigation had hit the proverbial wall, I decided to accept.

Chapter Twenty-Six

Walking into Miss Devin's cabin was like walking into a large fireplace. Scented smoke and the under-current of burning charcoal wafted around me.

"Do come in quickly, dear," she urged and pulled me in before slamming the door behind me. "We can't have the smoke escaping."

I coughed. "Of course not, Miss Devin. For then we'd let in too much fresh air, and that would never do."

"Exactly my point, Miss Knight. It delights me that we understand each other so well."

I responded with a series of hacking coughs. My eyes blurred with the sting of acrid smoke. "I didn't realize these cabins had fireplaces."

"They don't. This is all from my incense sticks

and some old newspapers. While my crystal ball isn't working this far away from land, my ability to read smoke hasn't been affected at all. Isn't that marvelous?"

"Brilliant." My teary eyes blinded by the smoke, I reached out my arms and felt for some solid surface with which to guide me. Following the wall, I winced when my knees banged into the edge of the bed. I sank onto the surface, grateful not to have to stand. "Is this healthy?"

"Oh, I very much doubt it. But what other option do I have? That silly little ghost of a man isn't going to leave me anytime soon unless I help him find his parrot."

I rubbed the tears out of my eyes. "About that—"

"And your presence here would be of great assistance to me."

"So we aren't having any dessert?"

"What an outrageous question. Of course we are, as soon as we find that poor man's bird and send him on his way."

"I'm not sure if that's the best idea," I said. "What will he do once he finds it?"

"That's between him and his thief of a wife. As

long as he's out of my closet by the time our dessert arrives, I don't much care."

"I appreciate the sentiment. I too have a ghost hiding in my cabin."

Miss Devin gasped. "Truly?"

"Yes. What is a woman to do these days?" I said. "It's bad enough they haunt us when they're alive, but it's quite a hassle when we have to contend with them after they die."

"You poor dear."

I refrained from saying anything more when a familiar form glimmered into view.

Gideon frowned as he looked around. "This isn't your cabin."

"Another one!" Miss Devin yelled as she sat next to me. "I shall have to deal with him as well. Have you also lost a parrot, young man?"

"No," Gideon said and gestured to his body. "But I do seem to have lost a body. Have you seen it anywhere?"

"Gideon, it's back in London, six feet underground," I said.

"You know this one?" Miss Devin asked.

"I once did. And it seems I will continue to do so."

She clucked her tongue in sympathy. "My dear

friend, you're far too young to be burdened with a ghostly suitor."

"I'm hardly a suitor," Gideon said. "I'm her—"

"Acquaintance," I said, not wanting to blow my cover. "We are acquaintances."

Gideon hissed and floated up to the ceiling, where he sulked and muttered to himself.

"If you want, I'll help you get rid of him afterward," Ms. Devin whispered.

I watched as Gideon circled around the ceiling, his outline disappearing and reappearing in billows of smoke. "Perhaps another time. I'm enjoying his company for now."

"That will change, Miss Knight. Mark my words. That will change. Now, are you ready to help me read the smoke?"

"I'm ready to get out of the smoke."

"That amounts to about the same thing. Hold my hands, and let's begin."

As I still hoped to receive dessert out of this exercise, I did as I was told. We grasped hands, and she began humming.

"What do you want me to do?" I whispered, hoping I wasn't interrupting her trance. The sooner she could finish, the sooner we could start breathing properly again.

"Focus on Mr. Twitcher," Miss Devin said.

"Right. I'm focusing. On what should I focus specifically? On his parrot? His eyepatch, peg leg—"

"Focus on anything, and say nothing," she said. "We're trying to summon him."

"Isn't he in the closet?"

"I need him here, inside the smoke."

I wasn't clear how it made any difference, but kept quiet and did as I was told. Perhaps the smoke assisted her to perform an exorcism of sorts, although this seemed to be a bit in reverse. We were summoning him, rather than sending him on his way.

The smoke billowed around us, and I began coughing in earnest.

"Miss Knight, do be quiet," Miss Devin said in between humming and murmuring strange words.

"I'm sorry, but I'm having difficulty breathing."

"Then hold your breath."

While I admired her willingness to prioritize her work over breathing, I felt in this case breathing wasn't overrated. And just before I considered breaking her hold on me and rushing out the door, Mr. Twitcher materialized in the space created by our connected arms.

"Gracious," I said and started to jerk backward.

Miss Devin's grip on my hands tightened. "Remain where you are, Miss Knight. Now we shall get to the bottom of this."

"Assuming we're still breathing by the end of this," I said.

"That will teach you," Gideon said from above me.

"Nobody asked you, Gideon," I said.

"What's he doing here?" Mr. Twitcher asked and glanced up at Gideon.

"Haunting me and being a nuisance," I said.

"Mr. Twitcher, I wish you to leave this ship and find peace," Miss Devin said.

I almost snorted, except I didn't have a lot of breath to spare. Since when did ghosts that remained in this dimension want peace? In my experience, ghosts stuck around because they wanted something along the lines of knowledge, revenge or entertainment. Then there were the mischievous ones who harassed and haunted their spouses.

But most ghosts I'd met didn't want peace in the sense of moving onward to wherever they were supposed to go. They were in fact quite content to loiter far beyond their expiry date.

"I'm not leaving until I find my parrot. Mrs. Twitcher owes me that much."

Miss Devin nodded, looking as if she actually cared about this ghost's feelings. "And why does she owe you anything, Mr. Twitcher?"

The man harrumphed, kicking his peg leg against the bed. Of course, the leg sank into the frame, thus depriving him of the satisfaction a good *thunk* gave a person. "She took my eye, my leg and eventually my life. The least she can do is give me back my pet."

Despite the stinging smoke, my eyes widened. "She murdered you?"

"I believe she did, young lady," Mr. Twitcher said and tipped his head toward me with a short bow. "One evening, I went to bed all well and good, at least as much as can be expected when I'm missing an eye and a leg. And the next morning, I didn't wake up. And more than that, she disappeared, taking with her my beloved bird. So what can be made of that?"

"It does seem a tad suspicious," I agreed and forced myself not to look up at Gideon. "Then again, appearances can be deceptive."

"What do you young ones know? She killed me, I'm telling you this. But am I asking for revenge?

Am I asking for an eye for an eye, a leg for a leg? No! I just want my parrot."

"And your parrot you shall have," Miss Devin said. "I shall consult with the smoke and inform you immediately regarding its location."

"I think we should skip this part and tell him to leave," I whispered.

"A promise is a promise!"

"You didn't actually promise him anything, and—"

"Hush now," Miss Devin said and gave me a stern look. "I'm going to help him."

The ghosts and I remained quiet as Miss Devin stared into the depth of the thick smoke. She hummed and nodded, wordlessly exclaimed and frowned. And just when I was about to pass out from lack of breath, she turned to Mr. Twitcher and said, "Sir, I have located your parrot."

The man smiled. Judging from the deeply entrenched wrinkles on his forehead, this was possibly his first smile in a very long time. "My delightful lady, that is indeed great news. And where is my beloved Sir Lancelot?"

"It's …" She paused and softly gasped.

"Where, woman, where?" Mr. Twitcher shouted.

She glanced past the ghost at me, realizing finally what I had tried to discreetly tell her. She swallowed hard, closed her eyes and said, "It's here on this very ship. It and your wife are down the hall."

Chapter Twenty-Seven

There was a pause in which I held out hope — faint and air-deprived — that the ghost of Mr. Twitcher had lost its hearing just as the man had lost an eye and a leg.

Alas, it was not to be. After a literally breathless moment of swirling incense and straining lungs, the ghost realized that the quarry he had long sought was only a few paces down the corridor from our current location. With a howl of rage similar to a declaration of war by a stampeding tribe of armed Celts, Mr. Twitcher became a smoky blur as he zoomed across the room and through the door.

"Aren't you going to lecture him about his rude manners?" Gideon asked.

"Not now, Gideon," I snapped, and stood up.

"Such a hypocrite. That's a double standard if I've ever seen one."

"What just happened?" Miss Devin asked.

"Chaos, that's what," I said and yanked open the door, almost collapsing at the gust of fresh air which assaulted my lungs.

"What a calamity. How was I to know his wife and parrot were both on board? What are the odds?" Miss Devin asked as she paused in the doorway.

"That's not the worst part," I said as I hurried after the ghost.

"What is?"

"Lancelot—"

"You mean Sir Lancelot."

I frowned over my shoulder and wondered why Mrs. Devin wasn't following me. "The parrot's dead. It's dead, stuffed and looks like it's experiencing a second death more painful than the first."

"Oh, my. I think I'll stay here and freshen up my room."

"Probably a good idea," I said and picked up the pace when Mr. Twitcher floated to a stop in front of Mrs. Twitcher's cabin.

"Sir, let's have a conversation about this, shall we?" I called out as I mentally went through my toolkit.

I had all manner of concoctions and gadgets to handle almost any creature of the paranormal and normal varieties. But ghosts were part of a rare category, being bodiless and all. I wasn't sure there was much I could do short of an exorcism, and I wasn't trained for that.

"You're a reasonable ghost, aren't you?" I asked, hoping to hear an affirmative.

"I'm going to kill her!"

"I guess not, then." I reached the cabin door just as Mr. Twitcher pushed himself through the wood. I yanked at the doorknob, but it was locked.

"What is it, dear ones?" Mrs. Twitcher asked just before a ruckus such as I've never heard exploded inside.

I was fairly certain she only had a dozen or so parrots in there, but it sounded as if there were a dozen flocks. Screeching and cawing accompanied by the flapping of wings assaulted my ears as I whipped out my lock pick set and began to work. I could only hope Mrs. Twitcher was blind to ghosts, as most humans were, and that Mr. Twitcher didn't have the energy to materialize in front of her.

"Who are you ... good heavens!" Mrs. Twitcher's exclamation was followed by a piercing scream to rival the cacophony of terrified parrots.

"So much for that hope," I said just as the lock clicked open, and I stumbled into the small room.

"Where's Sir Lancelot?" Mr. Twitcher demanded.

He was no longer a vague, smoky outline. He'd fully materialized and looked to be a fully fleshed, living man, even if only for a few moments. Ghosts could only materialize that strongly for short periods of time before they lost energy and faded away. But not before they wreaked havoc on the nerves of their victims. And that was precisely what was happening to Mrs. Twitcher.

The frail, elderly woman collapsed against the closet door, feeling for the doorknob as if she believed she could hide in there from the ghost of her dead husband.

"He was never your parrot, you foolish old man," she spluttered, gathering enough nerve despite her shock.

"You lying old hag!"

I was impressed Mrs. Twitcher was still upright and conscious. Many victims of a haunting would've used the opportunity to faint away rather than face an uncomfortable truth that the world of fantastical stories might have truth to it. But she was holding her own, and I realized she wasn't trying to open the closet door. She was making sure it stayed closed, which could only mean one thing: Sir Lancelot was still inside.

Mr. Twitcher must have come to the same conclusion. He howled his battle cry again and rushed toward his wife, who refused to move. He yanked at the door while she pressed her shoulder against it. They tussled back and forth as I tried to get Mr. Twitcher's attention.

"Help me, young lady," Mrs. Twitcher said while uselessly batting a feather against Mr. Twitcher's head. The feather sank into his head. She screamed and increased the force with which she battered him.

"There's not much I can do, Mrs. Twitcher, except to advise that you tell him the truth," I said, not hoping for much results from my sage advice.

"The truth? He's not ready for the truth!"

"What truth, you old hag? That you murdered me in my sleep?"

"You have made many nonsensical statements in my time, old man," Mrs. Twitcher yelled while pushing against the closet door. "And that isn't one of them."

He backed off, his energy starting to fade. "Ha! So you admit it? You admit you murdered me in order to steal my Sir Lancelot. I have a witness!"

"No, you ridiculous old fart. You died in your sleep. I left our home the next day to make arrangements for the funeral and to stay with my sister."

This admission further decreased Mr. Twitcher's energy until he was little more than an outline of a man.

Meanwhile, the parrots were still making an uproar. Too late, I realized that none of them were in locked cages or tied to their posts. Almost as if they shared a single mind, their heads turned to the open door behind me.

Mrs. Twitcher wailed, lifting up her hand as if to warn me. She stepped away from the closet door, and a triumphant Mr. Twitcher summoned enough energy to wrench it open. Sir Lancelot, stuffed and mangy, toppled off the shelf and straight through Mr. Twitcher's head.

The rest of the birds took that as a signal. I ducked as they bombarded me, but I was not their target. Instead, they dove straight through the entrance, into the passage and to freedom.

"Get them, you fool!" Mrs. Twitcher shouted.

"You murdered my parrot!" Mr. Twitcher howled.

"Oh, bother," I said.

Lying against the ceiling, Gideon howled with laughter, rocking back and forth as he wordlessly pointed at each one of us. I left him to his entertainment and hurried out into the corridor, bumping into Eleanor. She was clutching a tray with tea and an assortment of desserts, including chocolate pudding, destined no doubt for Miss Devin's room. I grabbed her before she could drop the tray.

"Miss Knight, what's all the—" She stopped talking, and her jaw dropped as she gazed at something behind me.

I spun around, then flung myself against the wall just as the flock of parrots veered toward us and away from a dead end.

Eleanor shrieked and tossed the tray in the air before dropping to the ground. Cutlery, chinaware and blobs of pudding floated upward just as feathers and squawking filled the air. The flock and the tea set collided in a colorful explosion. The macaw screamed, "Pretty boy, who's a pretty boy," as a film of chocolate pudding covered its back.

Gideon laughed hysterically, and I tried not to weep at the waste of a perfectly good dessert.

A billow of incense-scented smoke followed in the wake of the parrots as Miss Devin stepped out of her room. "Has our tea arrived yet, Miss Knight? I do hope so. My throat is rather parched."

Chapter Twenty-Eight

"What is ze meaning of zis?" an irritated voice in a thick French accent bounced toward me along with a pudding-smeared biscuit.

Miss Devin squeaked and hastily retreated into her room, tendrils of smoke flowing behind her.

"She released my parrots!" Mrs. Twitcher yelled and jabbed a bony finger at me.

Chief Officer Frenchy pounded down the stairs, his eyes ready to pop out of his skull. I was about to warn him of the dangers caused by stress when he inhaled and coughed heartily.

"You might want to wait up on the deck, sir," I suggested, hoping he would take the advice.

"What in ze" … *cough, cough* … "world are you" … *cough, cough* … "doing, Miss Knight?"

"Really, of all the nerve," I said. "Why would you think I have anything to do with this debacle?"

"She did, she did, sir," Mrs. Twitcher yelled. "My birds. My precious—"

"That you stole from me, you old hag," Mr. Twitcher shouted.

Fortunately, Chief Officer Frenchy was not the type of human who could detect paranormal elements and had no idea a ghost was shouting in his ear. The enraged ghost had expended his energy on manifesting in front of his wife and was now quite depleted. Nonetheless, I could unfortunately both hear and see him, even if the others could not.

"Wretched girl," Mrs. Twitcher muttered as she hobbled past me and followed the trail of feathers leading down the corridor, up the staircase and outside.

Chief Officer Frenchy scowled as he stomped toward me. "You and your supposed uncle. I knew you were troublemakers from ze start. Trouble! Zat's what I told ze captain. Zese two are trouble."

"In my defense, sir—"

"Zere is no defense. First, ze life rafts are inoperable. And now zis! What were you zinking, starting a fire in ze living quarters?"

"If I was going to start a fire, you would see the fire," I said.

For some reason, the chief officer wasn't impressed by my argument. "Zis is what happens when ze young women are left unaccompanied. You are hereby confined to your quarters."

"I beg your pardon?"

"You heard me." He waved a finger in front of my face, ignorant of the dangers of such behavior. I knew of several types of paranormals who would've snapped off that finger in one bite.

Just then, I caught sight of a ray of hope. While Eleanor had dropped the tray and much of the tea was now wasted, a piece of pie remained unsullied and perfectly whole on its plate.

"Confined, I tell you," Frenchy ranted. "I don't want to see you around."

"I assure you the feeling is quite mutual, sir," I said. "Watch where you put your step."

Sadly, the man wasn't inclined to listen to me. He continued his angry march down the corridor, inhaling deeply as he tried to track down the source of the smoke. His shiny black shoe landed on the piece of pie. He froze at the squelching sound made by the flaky pastry. Apple filling oozed out from under his sole.

He glanced down and muttered, "Merd."

"I agree. Such a waste of a perfectly decent pie," I said.

"Into ze cabin. Now!"

I huffed, more distressed by the demolished pie than by any threat Frenchy could offer. Under his glare, I returned to my cabin and slammed the door with a heavy thud.

"That was thoroughly satisfying," Gideon said in his whispery voice as he floated into the cabin after me.

"I should hardly think so. Mrs. Twitcher has lost her parrots, Mr. Twitcher has lost his mind, Miss Devin will quite likely never invite me over again, and I must now face the afternoon without tea or dessert. How is any of that satisfying?"

Gideon grinned. "Entertainment, my darling Beatrice. The entertainment value alone makes all other inconveniences worthwhile."

While I couldn't fault him for his logic, I wasn't about to admit that my current circumstances were anything but infuriating.

"Go out there and let me know if Frenchy is still around."

Gideon's eyes glittered with delight. "Are you going to break out of your confinement?"

"What a pointless question. Of course I am."

"And you give me permission to abandon—"

"Yes, Gideon. You don't need to ask each time if you have my blessing to be ill-mannered."

"One can never be sure, my dear."

My hands clenched around my walking stick. For a moment, I wished Gideon was alive and in his body long enough for me to thunk him over the head. "Noted. Now, please. Make yourself useful—"

"Me, useful? What a dreadful thing to say. The rights of the aristocrats and nobles are such that they needn't be useful at all. Usefulness is limited to teapots and horse carriages, not the likes of us."

"Truer words were never uttered by a ghost. Now off you go."

Laughing softly, Gideon did as I had instructed. A moment later, his head reappeared, looking as if someone had nailed it to the inside of my door. "All clear. Frenchy is around the corner, interrogating poor Miss Devin. At least he knows you didn't set a fire."

"Never fear, Gideon. There's still time left in the day to do so."

I glanced furtively in either direction, confirming Gideon's assessment of the situation.

Softly closing the door behind me, I dashed down the corridor. Mr. Twitcher was still raging about his dearly departed Sir Lancelot and all the other parrots his wretched, murderous wife stole from him. I did my best to ignore him, although Gideon paused to taunt him with a comment about the size of the parrot compensating for some aspect of … I stopped listening at that point.

I stepped onto the deck and ducked as the large macaw swooped dangerously close to my head. It settled on a railing, preened its glorious feathers and squawked, "Pretty boy, pretty boy, who's a pretty boy?"

Gideon huffed. "I am, of course. As if it has to ask, the blithering numskull."

"Pretty boy!"

A cool wind sliced against my cheek, causing me to shudder. I glanced up at the bruised sky. It looked like it was late evening rather than early afternoon. The choppy surface of the ocean mirrored the low-hanging, dark purple clouds. While I was no sailor, I suspected we were in for a rough night.

I stuffed my hands into my pockets to warm them up and paused when fingers brushed against cold metal. It was the pillbox, my key to normalcy or something resembling it.

"Now's not the time," I murmured and extracted my hands before the temptations of a normal life overcame me.

"What was that?" Gideon asked.

"Nothing." I started buttoning up my jacket and frowned at the long thread dangling from one of the buttons. "I do hope this isn't about to fall off," I complained as I plucked at the thread.

But it was no thread. It was a long, black hair. I reached into a pocket and retrieved the hair I'd found in cabin twenty-seven. I put them side by side on my palm. They were of the same length, texture and color.

"Whose are those?" Gideon asked with little interest. He was watching one of the younger female passengers stroll past us.

"She's not your type, as she's engaged to be married and isn't dead," I said. "As for the hairs, this one is from the cabin. But this other one was caught up in my button. And I wore this jacket when I was attacked in the engine room."

I looked up in time to see Gideon wave after the young woman who disappeared around the corner. Perhaps sensing my aggrieved gaze, he twirled around and performed an elaborate bow. "I'm all ears, beloved."

"This confirms my suspicions."

Gideon placed a hand over his heart. "I am nothing but faithful to you."

"Not you," I said and exhaled loudly. "Whoever attacked me has long, black hair. And I suspect this person is closely associated with a certain black cat who's now missing."

"I told you black cats are bad luck."

"They most certainly are not."

"In this case, they are."

"There is an exception to every rule. But do you know what this means?"

Gideon frowned. "We should go find you tea and chocolate post-haste?"

"An excellent deduction, and a brilliant option for later. I knew there was a good reason I married you."

"I'm sure I can think of a few bad reasons."

"As can I. I have a plan."

"I'm not going to like this, am I?"

I stroked the two strands of hair. "That depends. You might enjoy a tour of the lower levels of the ship."

"Will it involve running for your life?"

"Possibly."

He sighed. "Very well. But do try not to die, Beatrice. I'm not a fan of ship life."

"I'll do my best to remain alive, as I am rather attached to my body."

With that agreeable decision, I led the way down the stairs and toward the engine room.

Chapter Twenty-Nine

It wasn't difficult to persuade pirate Pip to accompany me into steerage.

"No," he initially shouted when I asked.

His loud voice accompanied with his intimidating physique would've caused most people to cower in fear. By now, I understood the perceived aggression was a result of the noisy environment and his concern for my well-being.

"I'm quite convinced my attacker is hiding in steerage," I explained. "And the attacker is the same person who stole an important object from my person. So you see, I can't very well leave this series of crimes unanswered."

Pip scowled. His craggy, scarred features formed a mask of rage which indicated he was thinking through my proposal. "I'll tells Rocky to catch your thief."

"And therein lies the one complication."

"Huh?"

"I'm not completely certain which person it is. There are at least two possible suspects and two or three potential accomplices."

He gawked at me a moment, his mouth agape, his eyes glazed. "You's mad, miss."

"I should hope so. Sanity isn't particularly useful in my line of work."

"What work?"

I tapped the end of my walking stick on the ground with little effect. The clanging, hissing and roar of the steam engine covered all other noises apart from its own.

"That's quite beside the point. Will you or will you not accompany me? For I mean to go to steerage and confront my suspects with or without you."

The man's great shoulders sagged in defeat. "Wait."

I retreated to the corridor and the relative silence. My ears were still buzzing from the assault of the engines when Pip walked out of the engine room, followed by his boss, Chief Engineer Rocky.

"Now what's this I hear, lassie?" Rocky exclaimed, his cheeks flushed with heat, irritation and possibly an overindulgence in liquid spirits.

"I haven't time to repeat the conversation," I said. "If you aren't willing to release Pip from his service for a few moments, then whatever results occur from my encounter with my suspects will be on your shoulders."

"You mean your very life and well-being is dependent upon my decision?"

I cleared my throat to swallow my laughter. "No, sir. The well-being of the *suspects* is dependent upon your decision. For either way, I shall be leaving the steerage in one piece, with my limbs intact, my heart still beating, and my lungs still functioning. I can't say the same for anyone else."

Rocky guffawed, slapping his thighs as he bent over double. "Oi, lass, I like your spirit. Pip, accompany her to ensure everyone leaves steerage on their own two legs. Except, of course, Miss Knight's assailant."

Still laughing at what he perceived to be a joke, he returned to the engine room. The hissing of steam punctured my hearing until the door slammed shut. Pip and I stared at each other.

"Does everyone refer to you as Miss Knight?"

Gideon asked, an angry sulk marring his features. "It's intolerable. And you say I'm rude for floating through walls."

I did my best to ignore the ghost's constant chatter about manners, propriety and my marital status as I led the way from engineering to steerage. We were climbing the last set of stairs when a pair of lovebirds fluttered into view.

"Odd," Pip said.

"Escaped parrots are the least of the oddities occurring on this ship. Don't mind the birds, but try not to step on the ghost," I said without thinking.

Pip stumbled over Mr. Twitcher's peg leg. Fortunately, Pip neither saw nor felt the ghost's presence, and he was blessed not to hear the volley of curses and threats which Mr. Twitcher flung at us as we reached the top of the steps.

"There be ghosts here?" Pip asked, clutching his hands together and shrinking away from the walls as if the ghosts were hiding in them.

"None with which you need concern yourself," I said. "Really, I don't understand how you lasted any length of time as a pirate."

"Peoples take one look at me, and they thinks the worst. I ain't never had to lift a sword against another."

I peered over my shoulder at him. "A useful skill, indeed. To win a fight without actually fighting bodes well for the continued maintenance of life and limb."

He shrugged and resumed studying the walls and ceiling as if anticipating a ghostly attack at any moment.

And this was why the Society's mandates included secrecy about the paranormal world. Most normal humans were simply not mentally robust enough to handle the truth. I silently castigated myself for the slip in protocol and determined not to mention such things again.

As we approached the door leading into the great hall for the steerage passengers, a commotion echoed toward us. Pip squeezed around me and blocked my passage with his wide back.

"Pip, this is hardly convenient if we wish to enter."

"Me first, miss. If you don't mind."

"I do mind, very much."

But being a man and a human, pirate Pip paid me no attention. Instead, he stepped forward, wrenched open the door and stepped into chaos.

Chapter Thirty

Ignoring Pip's warning to stay back, I slipped around the giant sailor and stared at the scene before me.

Somehow, the colorful macaw and two other parrots had made their way into the steerage level. Passengers were chasing them, making impromptu nets out of clothes in their efforts to capture the valuable birds.

The parrots, clearly possessing greater intelligence than some humans, had flown to the rafters. There they perched and made rude noises at the humans below.

The large macaw shrieked, "Pretty boy, who's a pretty boy," right before dropping a gift of sorts onto the long table. The bird's aim was impeccable.

Its deposit landed directly onto a tray of biscuits and looked like white icing.

The humans, not to be outdone by three birds, were now organizing themselves. One of them lifted up a chair and placed it on the table, but was still unable to reach the rafters. Other passengers were arguing about who should benefit from the capture. None of them were paying any attention to us or my suspects.

"Those are my parrots," Mr. Twitcher shouted as he appeared at my side.

Not surprisingly, the humans were oblivious to his presence, except the old woman in the far corner. She nudged the young woman Delilah, and they both gawked at the ghost who began shouting at the humans while trying to coax his pets onto his shoulders.

The old woman's gaze drifted past the enraged ghost and settled on me. I squinted my eyes at her. When it came to the work of the Society, I had to set aside propriety and manners in favor of results. And this was precisely why I wanted to retire. That, and the risk my position posed to longevity and retention of all my limbs.

Keeping to the edge of the chaos, I jogged down the length of the hall, my squinted gaze never leaving the two women and the three girls. Pip followed me, his boots thudding heavily, his loud exhale brushing over my head.

"Leave my birds alone, you rabble! You fiends. You devious parrot snatchers," Mr. Twitcher screamed.

"Who's a pretty boy. Who's a pretty boy."

"Miss, maybe this ain't the best time to be here," Pip huffed.

"Why ever not?"

"The parrots. The people. I think—"

I didn't hear what Pip thought. My attention was primarily focused on the five suspects, because I had now included the girls on that list. All five of them had strange signals in their energy fields. And while I couldn't quite decipher the meaning, I knew one thing for certain: these women were not normal humans. In fact, I had my suspicion as to what they really were, but wouldn't be able to confirm it until I was close enough to use my spectacles.

And of course, the women were as equally determined that I never get close enough to do so. With alarmed expressions, the two women herded the three girls to the other side of the hall. From there, they began to run the length of the room, heading toward the chaos and the exit on the other side of the excited crowd.

"Curses," I muttered and spun around, only to collide with Pip.

The impact did nothing to stop his momentum but sent me flying backward and skidding a few feet on my bottom. It was a thoroughly undignified position for anyone, particularly a paranormal investigator who was on the heels of her quarry.

"Apologies, miss," Pip gushed as he reached down to pull me up.

"What a scoundrel," Gideon hissed in my ear.

"Death to the parrot snatchers!" Mr. Twitcher yelled.

"Gracious, this is pure pandemonium." I waved Pip's hand away as I stumbled to my feet and ran toward the doorway. The five women had already exited the hall and were racing down the corridor.

"They ain't gonna go far, miss," Pip reassured me as we dashed past the parrot-chasing mob.

"Don't be so sure," I said and ducked out of the hall just in time to see one of the girls change into a black cat.

Chapter Thirty-One

"That girl," Pip shouted. "She ain't ... did she ... she's a cat!"

It turned out my pirate friend possessed more imagination than I had given him credit for.

I shook my head. "What girl? Let's focus on what's important, Pip. Apprehending those thieves!"

My attempt at distraction succeeded. The man ceased worrying about the very obvious if not peculiar situation of an adolescent child turning into a cat, and the captain's cat, no less.

The older woman said something to the others, and one of the girls scooped up the cat and continued to run toward the stairs leading to the outer deck. Meanwhile, the old woman turned and blocked our passage, her dark eyes glinting dangerously.

"Right," I muttered and skidded to a halt. "Of course she wants to resist capture. Why can't they ever come quietly?"

"She ain't nothin' but an old lady," Pip said, thus proving he was a human of limited imagination after all.

The woman hissed, as if she understood very well the insult delivered to her in a foreign language. She bent her hands into claws. Her nails lengthened until they were sharpened talons.

"Perhaps you should let me handle this, Pip. Woman to woman, so to speak."

I didn't have to look at Pip to sense his mood. He was hesitating over the whole situation. A pirate he might be, but he was a gentleman nonetheless. He was still treating the old woman as an old woman instead of the paranormal she really was.

"If you really think so—"

"I definitely do. Perhaps you could assist Mr. Twitcher—"

"Who?"

"Did I say mister? I meant *Mrs.* Twitcher. Those parrots are hers."

"They are not!" Mr. Twitcher shouted from

behind me. How he managed to overhear me with all the chaos was a mystery I didn't wish to dwell on.

"Stop intruding in my conversations, Mr. Twitcher," I shouted over my shoulder.

The cranky old ghost scowled before retreating back into the hall.

Pip hurried away from me, and I waited until he was back in the hall before reaching for my blow gun tucked into a small drawer of my walking stick.

"Girl witch," the old woman said, her eyes shifting into that of a cat.

"There's no need to be rude," I said. "If you'd just come along quietly, we can have a civilized conversation of sorts. Or better yet, return my pyramid, and I'll forget all about this little misunderstanding. What say you?"

The cat woman snarled, her canines elongating.

"I see. So that's how you want it, do you?"

She lowered herself into a crouch, as if about to pounce. As long as she remained either in this old woman form or that of a small house cat, I wasn't too concerned. In fact, I rather hoped she did change into another Cairo. Although I wasn't a fan of cats, they were easier to handle than a panther.

She stalked toward me, still in a crouch, her yellow eyes fixed on me. "It's not yours."

"Wonderful! You speak English. As for the pyramid, it certainly isn't yours," I said. "I intend to deliver it to its rightful owner. Now do stop making a fuss and hand it over. I've missed my dessert, and the lack of sugar has left me in a foul mood."

The woman growled. Really, the atrocious manners of the paranormal elements never ceased to amaze me. It was one thing to have the power to shift forms. But that was no excuse for using animal sounds while in human form.

I held up the dart gun and inserted a fresh dart. "You really leave me no choice. I hope you understand. This only goes to show what happens when you interrupt my tea."

The woman had had enough. She launched her attack before I could finish my sentence — yet another display of unacceptably bad manners. Fortunately, the dart was prepared. I blew into the gun just as something pummeled me from behind.

"Who's a pretty boy?" the macaw shrieked as it climbed onto my head.

The force of its impact jolted my aim and sent my dart flying wildly overhead. The old woman cackled as she jumped at me.

"Of all the wretched luck," I said.

It was a good thing I never relied solely on my tools. In my experience, the most reliable of weapons was the one that didn't look like a weapon: my walking stick. Still fuming at the manner in which Lady Luck had treated me, I rolled with the woman and managed to free myself from her grip. Standing up, I swung my stick like a bat, connecting not too delicately against the back of her head.

With a howl, she fell to her knees, then collapsed across the corridor, quite unconscious.

"I did warn you. This is what inevitably happens when one crosses with a Society agent," I said and hurried after the other cat people.

Chapter Thirty-Two

I knew we were in trouble when I exited the steerage section and reached the open deck.

The storm which had threatened the ship for the past few days had unleashed itself upon us. Wind howled with such strength that it almost succeeded in pushing me back inside. As it was, I had to lean against the outer wall to retain my balance.

The waves were now high enough to slosh some of their burden across the ship's lower decks, and sheet lightning lit up the purple sky. The thunder crashed immediately afterward.

"Miss Knight!"

I turned, half-expecting to see a ghost or a parrot or perhaps a shifting cat-woman. Instead,

Eleanor, my young sailor friend, stood before me. "Have you not heard, miss? The captain has given orders that all passengers are to return to their quarters immediately. They're not to exit until given further notice. It's not safe out here."

"It's hardly safer inside," I said, searching the deck for any sign of a cat or the shifter women. "You haven't seen any cats around, have you?"

"No, but don't worry about Cairo. Cats always take care of themselves."

"That's what I'm afraid of."

"Ey, you," a French voice yelled. It was loud enough to be heard above another rumble of thunder. "I zought I told you to stay in your cabin. Do you want to join your uncle in ze brig?"

Eleanor flinched, but I did my best to ignore Chief Officer Frenchy. Really, the man was such a nuisance, always appearing at the most inconvenient moments and asking what were obviously rhetorical questions. Why did people do that? It really was a bother and an inconvenience.

"Do you hear me, mademoiselle? Return to your quarters at once. Or else a great wave will toss you overboard. Not zat I shall miss your presence. But ze captain has an unfortunate policy of delivering *all* his passengers to ze destination."

Frenchy appeared thoroughly distressed by the captain's enlightened policy. I couldn't entirely blame him. I had similar feelings in regards to some of the individuals I had to handle in my line of work.

He didn't bother to see if I would follow his instructions, perhaps secretly wishing I wouldn't. Instead, he snapped an order at Eleanor to continue her rounds. He then hurried inside to harass some other unsuspecting person.

I waited for him to disappear out of sight before continuing my tour of the lower deck.

"Miss Knight—"

"Don't worry about me, Eleanor," I said. "I've managed more foul beasts than Frenchy."

"But I warrant you haven't seen such rough seas before."

She wasn't wrong, but I had no time to explain. Because at that moment, I caught sight of my suspects.

"Now why would they do that?" I muttered as I hurried toward one of the sabotaged life rafts.

One of the girls saw me approach and shouted at her mother. The mother ignored her and continued to lower the life raft off the edge of the ship.

"You'll drown," I shouted as I increased my stride. "This is not the time to make a great escape."

The woman only worked faster, and I wondered what she hoped to achieve apart from a watery demise.

The cat seemed to have more sense, for it wiggled out of its sister's arms and leaped onto the deck. The mother shouted and started to climb out of the life raft, but it was too late. One of the winches suddenly snapped, and the life raft plunged downward at an awkward angle. While I could no longer see them, their cries penetrated through the raging storm.

"Of all the incompetent, selfish behaviors," I muttered. "Now I suppose you expect me to rescue you."

The cat pounced on my boots, its little claws attempting to sink through the leather. It stared up at me, meowing pitifully.

"Very well, but you owe me an explanation and a favor. Are we clear?"

The cat slunk away from me but not too far. I decided that was about as much of an agreement as I could possibly expect from a feline and went to the railing over which the life raft had fallen.

Fortunately, whatever sabotage Prof. Runal had inflicted, it was only enough to disable part of the winch system. The raft hung a few feet below the edge of the deck, one of its ends closer to the hungry waves than the other. The woman and two of her daughters were holding onto one of the ropes connecting the raft to the ship. The whole situation looked precarious.

"Don't move," I shouted. "And don't pretend like you don't understand me. Wretched paranormal people."

"Do they have one of my birdies?" Mr. Twitcher asked as he leaned over the rail next to me.

"As you can clearly see … Yes, in fact they do. And if you wish me to retrieve your avian pet, I suggest you go back into the steerage hall and request Pip to come out here and help me."

"The scurvy thieves," Mr. Twitcher said. "They won't get away so easily this time."

"That's the spirit. Now off you float."

While Mr. Twitcher went away — hopefully to convince Pip to come outside — I searched the deck for anything that might be remotely useful. A round lifebuoy hung from a hook on the wall. It included a length of rope that looked like it was long enough to reach the women. Whether it was strong enough to hold all three of them was another matter entirely.

"It's better than nothing," I said just as a particularly aggressive wave pummeled the side of the ship. The entire vehicle lilted to one side, and I lost my balance in the ensuing change in gravity. The wall was temporarily the floor, and by the time the ship managed to right itself, I feared the worst.

Removing the lifebuoy from its hook, I hurried to the edge of the railing and peered over cautiously. The life raft was now vertical, hanging by only one rope. A heavy, salt-filled mist momentarily blinded me. In the haze, it seemed the women had been washed into the ocean from which there would be no rescue. But when the wave retreated, I saw them huddled on the tip of the life raft and holding onto the one remaining rope.

I tied one end of the lifebuoy's rope to the railing, checked the knot, then tossed it at Delilah. I was congratulating myself for my aim when the lifebuoy landed around the woman's neck. Startled, she almost lost her grip but managed to hold on. She took off the safety device and placed it around one of her daughters, then urged the other one to hold on. She then looked up at me and gestured for me to pull. I tried, but the weight of all three of them was too much.

Perhaps discerning this truth, she let go of the lifebuoy to the accompaniment of her daughters' screams.

"Here, miss. I got it," a deep voice rumbled next to me.

Never was I more grateful to see a pirate. Together, we hauled up the two girls. They collapsed on the deck, not willing or able to stand as the ship rocked back and forth.

"There's one more," I said.

Pip leaned over the railing, then frowned at me. "Ain't no one else."

Gasping in horror, I joined him and scanned the lifeboat. Delilah was nowhere to be seen.

Chapter Thirty-Three

I escorted the girls — two in human form, one as a cat — into the empty cabin they'd been using to access the first-class level. Given that all of the passengers had now retreated to their quarters, and the crew was too occupied keeping the ship afloat to monitor the comings and goings of steerage passengers, no one challenged their right to be in cabin number twenty-seven.

I deposited the cat onto the bed, then indicated for the girls to make themselves comfortable. They were soaked and dripping ocean water all over the floor, but I didn't dare leave them unguarded to find dry clothing for them.

"Now I must know the truth," I said. "Who are you, and where—"

"Our mama," one of the girls wailed, then burst into tears.

"Good heavens," I muttered as I searched the cabin for a piece of cloth I could give her to dry her tears. This was precisely why I had no intention of entering into the family way, even if it was a possibility for me. Finding not a scrap of cloth, I settled for offering my own handkerchief.

She stared at it, then at me in confusion. "Cold." She shivered and rubbed her wet sleeves.

I gave up. "Stay in here. If you try to escape, I will find you and lock you up in the brig. Do you understand?"

I didn't like resorting to harsh tones, but I had neither the energy nor patience to negotiate for their compliance. The two young ladies nodded, and the cat meowed.

Taking that as agreement, I stepped outside the room and sighed wistfully at the squashed apple pie with the outline of Frenchy's shoe imprinted into it.

The ship tilted dramatically back and forth, and the plate with the crushed dessert slid past me as if to mock my desires.

"Heavens, now the ocean works against me." I hurried a few cabins down and knocked on Miss Devin's door.

She warily opened and gasped at the sight of me. I could only imagine what she saw. The wind had wreaked havoc on my hair, yanking it out of the bun in which I kept it. My jacket was drenched with salty water and a few scraps of sea plants. I probably stunk like a fishmonger's shop.

"I have no time to explain, Miss Devin," I said. "In cabin twenty-seven, there are two girls and a cat in need of your administration. Some warm, dry clothes would be most appreciated."

"The cat requires clothes as well?"

It was a fair question, and I was impressed by her ability to focus on the important matters. "I doubt it, but bring along an extra sweater, a blanket and towels if you don't mind. I'm off to find another one."

"Another cat or another blanket?"

"Probably both. And it wouldn't hurt if I could find a cup of tea somewhere on the ship."

I left her to look after the girls while I returned to steerage. Pip had followed my instructions and was assisting the old woman to stand. Her claws had retracted into normal human nails, and she was still groggy from the wallop she'd received.

"Well done, Pip. I'll take her from here."

He looked skeptical. "You sure, miss?"

I took a few breaths before answering while the old woman muttered something unsavory about human males and their limited ability to think creatively about females. I sympathized with her sentiments. Despite all that Pip had witnessed, he persisted on treating me like a frail, delicate woman in need of a man's protection. Not that he hadn't been helpful, mind you. But there were limits to how much assistance a man could provide, particularly in such circumstances.

"My dear Pip, I assure you I shall manage just fine. Perhaps you'd be kind enough to help secure the parrots?"

"Maybe later. Rocky'll need me help, or we ain't gonna survive the storm."

"I approve of your priorities. By all means, we wouldn't want the engine to fail us now."

We parted ways, and I escorted the old woman back into first class. She gave me only her first name — Alexander — and showed no interest in knowing my name. Instead, she gawked at the extravagance around her as we proceeded down the passage to the cabin in which her granddaughters waited.

"One room for the whole family?" she asked.

"Actually, most of these rooms only have one occupant."

Alexander wrinkled her face and spat onto the floor. "Such a waste of space."

"You could be right. I must inform you of an unfortunate incident," I said. "Delilah didn't make it."

"What?"

"I tried to save her, but the ocean took her."

Instead of sagging to the ground or collapsing into heart-wrenching sobs, the old woman cackled. "Not likely."

"Really, it's the truth."

"I don't believe it."

"I'm so sorry," I said. "I did try, but the storm was too rough."

As if to prove the point, a giant wave pummeled the ship's side, and we lurched into the closest wall, banging heads and arms against each other.

"She will find a way," Alexander said. "My Delilah, she always lands on her feet."

"Given what she is, I can believe that," I said. Even though I wasn't one to normally give false reassurances, I also didn't want to deal with all of the tears which were certain to follow if I shared my true assessment of the situation.

I didn't argue, as my attention was caught elsewhere. "Oh, pox and curses," I said when I saw a black cat dart away from the door to cabin twenty-seven and race down the corridor away from me. "It seems one of your girls has decided to go exploring."

I yanked open the door and entered the cabin, preparing to lecture Miss Devin. There was no need to do so. The three girls, all in human form now, jumped off the bed and launched themselves into their grandmother's arms.

Miss Devin smiled. "I love family reunions. But I didn't find a cat in here, Miss Knight. Perhaps it slipped out."

"Perhaps."

Alexander gloated over the girls' heads. "That cat we saw was Delilah. I told you she survived."

"So it would seem. However—"

The girls burst into cheers.

I frowned at them until they settled down. "I'm happy for your daughter—"

"Granddaughter," Alexander said. "These girls are my great grandchildren."

"I must commend you on your skincare regime," I said. "Perhaps we could exchange recipes. My aunt would be most grateful. As for Delilah, I need to have a word with her. Now that you're all back together—"

"Not all of us," Alexander corrected.

"Most of you, and that's no small feat," I said. "I must insist you return the object you stole from me."

Alexander's features wrinkled up in bemused confusion. "Which object?"

One of the girls leaned toward her and whispered.

"Ah. That one. It's difficult for me to keep track of these things. The pyramid. We don't have it."

"But surely—" I began.

"My granddaughter Delilah stole it from you," Alexander continued. "If you want your pyramid back, you will have to find her."

"What a party, and why wasn't I invited?" Gideon asked as he floated through the door.

The girls shrieked, then giggled as Gideon did a pirouette followed by an elaborate bow.

"Strange company," Alexander said and peered at me.

"They get stranger all the time," I agreed.

"By the way, my darling," Gideon said. "I thought you might like to know that Chief Officer Frenchy is inspecting all of the first-class quarters to make sure everyone is in their place."

"That is most inconvenient of him," I said.

"Not to mention inconsiderate, too, for what will he say when he sees my cabin is empty, and this one full of people who aren't supposed to be here?"

Gideon's smile widened. "I'm not sure, but I suspect we're about to find out."

A heavy thump landed on the door. "Who's in zere?"

I cringed. But great grandmother Alexander didn't hesitate. She ushered the girls to one side of the door, then gestured for me to open it. I in turn gestured to Miss Devin.

"He hates me," I whispered.

"He really does," Gideon said. "Just now, I heard him muttering about you. Something about throwing you in the brig or over the railing. I wasn't quite sure which one. Maybe both."

"That's not very helpful, Gideon," I said.

"I was merely agreeing with your assessment. Isn't that what husbands are supposed to do?"

"Among other things," I said and indicated to the confused Miss Devin to open the door while I huddled with the cat women against the wall.

Obediently, Miss Devin cracked the door open ever so slightly.

"Madam, what are you doing in zere?" Frenchy

asked, his irritation mixing with the salty dampness of my clothes to grate against my skin.

"This is my cabin, isn't it? It isn't? Oh, dear. I was so confused, so startled by the storm," she said, her deep, rumbling voice mixing with Gideon's hysterical cackle.

"How is zis confusing? Zis is number twenty-seven right here. You see? You should be in ze cabin down ze hall."

"You're quite correct, sir. But you understand how frail a woman's nerves can be."

His harrumph didn't deny her comment, and I wasn't sure whether to cheer Miss Devin's creative manipulation of men's natural prejudices against women, or slam the door in that man's arrogant face. I decided the former option would be best, given that I didn't want to spend the remainder of the trip in the brig.

"I must ask you to return to your cabin immediately. You can't remain in zere."

"But it's so scary in my cabin," she wailed. "I'll be all alone. The waves! I feel like I'm about to drown in there."

Frenchy mumbled a series of unsavory comments in French.

"I'm sorry," Miss Devin said. "I don't speak German."

"Merd!"

He finally left after extracting a promise that she would return to her own quarters as soon as she felt comfortable to do so.

Miss Devin closed the door, her expression changing from meek and terrified to self-satisfied. "Men. They're so easy to fool."

"Well done, my dear," I said. "I'll leave these ladies in your capable hands."

"And where are you going?"

"To see if I can find a cat and a pyramid."

Chapter Thirty-Four

Trying to keep upright proved to be a difficult task. By the time I caught a glimpse of a black cat, my shoulders ached from the numerous encounters with the walls. Nonetheless, I persisted and followed Delilah's feline form all the way to the other end of the first-class level and into the dining room.

The room was uncharacteristically dark and empty, as the crew had pushed all the tables and chairs over to one side and secured them so they couldn't move with the ship's to and fro. I paused at the doorway, squinting my eyes in the hopes I could pick up on Delilah's energy before she pounced on me. The flicker of a small, feline form alerted me to her presence.

"There's no point in hiding, Delilah," I said.

With an angry hiss, she dashed across the room and into the kitchen.

"Come now. Can't we discuss this over a cup of tea? Let me know if you find any pudding in there. All this running about on an empty stomach isn't healthy, you know."

The only response was the slap of sea spray against the window. The view was momentarily obstructed by ocean foam, and it didn't improve much when the wave retreated.

"Gracious. The inconveniences I must endure."

I marched after the cat and paused at the kitchen's entrance to stare into the unlit room. Dark shadows outlined the counter and appliances. I could see nothing else, yet sensed movement.

My hesitation most likely saved my life. A blade sunk into the doorframe precariously close to my ear with a dull thud. I squatted before the second knife could lodge itself in my chest.

"There's really no need for this, Delilah. Why don't we sit down and have a civilized conversation. Woman to cat, so to speak."

"Stay away from us!" Delilah shrieked before hurling another steak knife at me.

By that time, I'd already retreated into the dining room. I crouched next to the doorway, marveling at how a cat could have such good aim.

"I really need that pyramid back."

"It's not theirs, you know," Delilah shouted.

"And I suspect it's not yours, either. Is it?"

Thunder and lightning interrupted our conversation, and we both waited for the storm to quiet a bit before we continued.

"I'm taking it to the rightful owner," Delilah said.

"What a coincidence. I am as well."

"Ha! You're taking it to the Egyptian government, not the owner."

The ship rolled from side to side so steeply that I slid toward the huddle of tables and chairs. Something crashed in the kitchen, and I only hoped Delilah wasn't too incapacitated. I needed her to answer my questions.

"Before we die, I would very much like to know the whereabouts of the pyramid," I shouted.

"Absolutely not," Delilah said. "Hey! Who are you?"

"Did you steal my parrots?"

"Mr. Twitcher, your timing is dreadful," I said.

"I don't much appreciate you interrupting our conversation."

"Hey, cat! We're not finished. Come back here. I'm talking to you," the ghost said and flew into the dining room, hovering above a small, black shape.

A door slammed against a wall. Chief Officer Frenchy entered and stooped to pick up the cat. "Zere you are, you wretched beast."

Delilah hissed and tried to scratch his face, but it seemed Frenchy was quite familiar with the ways of cats. He held Delilah by the scruff of her neck. Her paws scratched harmlessly at the air.

"It's a conspiracy, I tell you," Mr. Twitcher moaned.

"And what are you doing here, Miss Knight?" Frenchy demanded when I stood and approached him.

"I suspect the same as you," I said and snatched the cat from him before he could protest. "I was terribly worried about Cairo, you see. I have a fondness for the little kitty. I'll take care of it. I'm sure you are far too busy and far too important to be looking after a cat, after all."

Frenchy puffed out his chest. "Quite right, mademoiselle. I told ze captain ze cat is fine, but he insisted I search for it. I zought it was hiding out in one of ze cabins. It has put me through a lot, I tell you."

"And now you can inform the captain the cat is in very good hands. Good evening, sir. And if it's not asking for too much, could I order some room service?"

Lightning crackled across the sky, illuminating Chief Officer Frenchy's scowl.

"You are most lucky I'm too busy to escort you to ze brig, Miss Knight," Frenchy said. "Let zis be your last warning." He spun on a heel and left the dining room in the direction of the bridge where he would no doubt update the captain on his successful mission and Cairo's good health.

I waited for him to disappear up the stairs before hurrying to the first-class quarters. The whole time, I clutched the cat to my chest, keeping her immobile. "And if you try to claw my eyes out, I assure you I will make good use of this walking stick," I warned when she squirmed.

The moment I entered the very crowded cabin twenty-seven, I dropped Delilah to the ground. She at once transformed into her human self and was bombarded by her children. It was a touching scene, if one was predisposed to maternal sentiments. Fortunately, I didn't suffer from any such afflictions. I was more irked than anything else.

"Now, let's have the truth," I said.

Miss Devin pulled out an incense stick from the front of her dress. "And while we're at it, a little bit of smoke to set the mood."

Chapter Thirty-Five

As Miss Devin lit her incense stick, Delilah and Alexander sat on the bed. The three girls dropped to the floor in a semicircle around their mother and great grandmother. I remained standing, walking stick in hand on the off chance one of the women decided to become a little too frisky for her own good. Miss Devin took the room's one chair, her bulk filling it completely.

"Now, I believe I'm owed an explanation," I said.

Alexander scoffed. "You are owed nothing, Miss Knight, agent of the Society for Paranormal Suppression."

"That's not the Society's full name," I said. "I can't abide by such inaccurate statements."

Delilah crossed her arms over her chest and narrowed her eyes at me. But my attention was on her grandmother, the matriarch of this little band.

"Think what you might, child," Alexander said. "But I tell you this. You are mistaken about the pyramid."

We paused to allow the crashing thunder to fade. Miss Devin held out her incense stick like a wand and waved it overhead, and I blinked at the acidic tinge of the smoke.

"Do you know what that pyramid really is?" Delilah asked.

"A puzzle. And I suspect there's a key within."

I was gratified to observe surprise on Delilah's face and a reluctant nod of approval from Alexander.

"Do you know what the key is for?" Delilah persisted, not satisfied to let me win a round.

"I'm not as certain on that point," I admitted. "Only that it's vital for maintaining the interests of the British Empire and its Egyptian allies."

"This is so terribly exciting," Miss Devin said as she stood and tipped the incense stick over my head, sprinkling a bit of ash on my nose in the process. "In the future, I shall venture out of my cabin more often."

"If it's excitement you seek, human, then be prepared for your wish to be granted," Delilah snarled.

"How titillating," Miss Devin said, then went silent when I gave her a stern look.

"You are right. It's a puzzle which contains a key," Alexander said. "But it will not be used to end a war. The Sudanese are already as good as defeated. They just don't know it yet. And in the grand scheme of things, that war is more of a skirmish between men. No, the pyramid and its contents will be used for a far more nefarious goal."

"More dastardly than the defeat of a nation?" I asked.

"Yes. The pyramid holds the key to an ancient weapon that can be mobilized against the energy of a paranormal." Alexander paused and studied me, as if assessing my ability to grasp the importance of her statement. "I don't know what you think about your own true nature, Miss Knight. But I assure you that you are no more worthy of life than we are."

Before I could ask her to explain the strange statement, she pressed on. "It is possible you are innocent of malicious intent, but there are others in your organization and outside of it that are less motivated by pure intentions. It's for this reason we are prepared to drown ourselves in the ocean rather than allow a Society operative to deliver the key into the wrong hands."

"And you are so certain that those hands are wrong?" I asked and squinted, searching for a trace of the lie that must be there. I found none.

Both Alexander and Delilah nodded their heads in unison.

Another series of waves buffeted the ship like it was a toy in a child's bathtub. One of the girls whimpered and leaned herself against her mother's legs. Delilah's features softened, and she stroked the child's head until the girl relaxed.

"Why should I believe you?" I asked, even though I already did. They weren't lying, and what they said made more sense than the story Prof. Runal had given me. "Why should I believe you have loftier motivations than the Director of the Society himself?"

Delilah frowned, but Alexander answered. "I do not question your motivation or that of the werewolf."

Miss Devin gasped, and I glanced over to ensure she wasn't going to faint away. But instead, her eyes were open and glittering with curiosity, completely absorbed by the story unfolding before her. "Werewolves. Imagine that!"

"I do my best not to," I said and wondered how much of the truth Prof. Runal knew and had concealed from me.

Alexander continued, "I know how the world works. Believe me when I say I'm a lot older than you, Miss Knight. And I swear to you on my life, and the life of my granddaughter and great grand-daughters, that what I have said is in fact the truth. Delilah, the pyramid."

She held out her hand, ignoring Delilah's protests. Hissing, Delilah reached into her robes and pulled out the small pyramid.

"Perhaps you have learned how to open this puzzle?" Alexander asked and gave me the pyramid.

"No," Delilah said, then added harsh words in that unique language of theirs.

But Alexander held up her hand, and Delilah fell silent.

"Yes, I believe I have figured it out," I said. "But perhaps you would do the honors."

I handed the pyramid back to Alexander, who smiled. With a quick series of twists, she revealed the outline of the puzzle. Another couple of turns, and the top portion of the pyramid slid to one side, revealing a small chamber cleverly built into the wooden blocks. And inside that chamber was a key that looked as ancient as the Great Pyramid of Giza itself.

"And now, Miss Knight. What do you suggest we do?"

I pulled my gaze away from the intricately designed key and puzzle, and met Alexander's unwavering gaze. "I suggest I complete the Society's mission and return the pyramid to the supposedly rightful owners. And you can return the other item to its owner."

I couldn't help gloating a little bit when Alexander and Delilah shared matching expressions of surprise.

"So you won't keep the key?" Alexander asked.

I plucked up the pyramid and upended it over her open palms. "What key?"

The key glowed against her dark skin as we stared at each other. Then Alexander tucked the key inside her robe with a smug expression only a cat could possess.

Chapter Thirty-Six

"My dear Beatrice, my clever Miss Knight, my brilliant young protégé," Prof. Runal bellowed after I'd discreetly given him the good news. "I knew you would succeed where the fates doomed others to fail."

I glanced around the brig. Lady Larrona and Lord Voleur had given up on trying to convince me to break them free. Lord Voleur was toying with a deck of cards while Lady Larrona glared mental daggers at me.

"We may need to use circumspection, sir," I said in a soft tone. "Chief Officer Frenchy is looking for an excuse to toss me into the brig with you."

"Poppycock! Rubbish! Nothing to worry about.

Let me see it, then." He rubbed his large hands together, the skin scraping loudly.

We were still separated by bars, as Frenchy had made it abundantly clear he would not be releasing the professor until we reached land.

"And if he causes us more trouble, I shall throw him back into ze brig," Frenchy added before allowing me a short visit.

Careful to keep my back to the hostile gaze of the museum thieves, I pulled out the small pyramid and held it on my palm for him to admire.

"Well done, Beatrice. I never had a doubt. Not one. We shall soon hand it over to the appropriate authorities and be done with it."

I dropped the pyramid into my purse and nodded my approval of the plan. "Will we need to disembark? If we can at all avoid it, I would be quite relieved."

I didn't allow myself a shudder of concern, but I couldn't help think about the last time I had stood upon the African continent. Whatever Prof. Runal might say, Egypt was a part of Africa. And my previous experience in Lagos hadn't left me with a favorable impression.

Prof. Runal nodded several times, his great

mane of hair bouncing back and forth. "Be at ease, Beatrice. Do not fret one bit. For the captain has agreed to allow our contact person to briefly come aboard. The exchange can be made right here. In this very location."

"In the brig, sir? You're going to entertain a guest here?"

The professor's laugh boomed through the space, filling it with a joyful buoyancy that normally wouldn't be found in the ship's prison. "Oh, no. *He* shall be entertaining *us*, I'm quite sure. Besides, we are merely transferring the object from one hand to the other. And then, our mission is done, complete and finished. You've deserved quite a holiday, my dear. A vacation, if I might be so bold to say."

This time, I didn't try to repress the shudder. "If you don't mind, sir. I think I'm quite done with vacations for a while."

"But don't you want to see the real pyramids? It's only a short excursion from the port, or so I've been told."

"I've seen enough of pyramids as well, sir. I would be just as satisfied for us to remain on ship and return immediately to London."

"And a good thing, too," he said. "For your dear

friend the chief officer has decided he won't release me except to the London authorities. Good thing we have a vampire or two in our employment in that fair city who can sort things out with the English police."

Our plan thus decided, I bid him good day and wandered around the ship. After yesterday's storm, the morning had dawned in glorious fashion with all the sunshine the professor had promised me, and a calm, flat sea.

The cat women remained as my guests in the first-class cabin. Gideon had somehow convinced Mr. Twitcher to keep an eye on the passage and alert us if Chief Officer Frenchy dared return. But he had no need to, because by some miracle, Cairo had taken up her position with the captain. The girls took it in turns to be the captain's favorite passenger. As he had no other concerns with first-class quarters, he didn't request Frenchy to investigate any further.

Alexander still decried the waste of space and the sheer opulence. Delilah told her to keep quiet and enjoy it while they could. I preferred to spend my days on deck, fresh air and sunshine being in limited supply both in my quarters and back in London.

One evening during dinner, the ship slowed as the engine spluttered and ceased to work.

"Now what?" Mrs. Spratt demanded.

Eleanor, who was waiting on my table, looked out the window and grinned. "We're approaching the canal. We're almost there."

"Well, we couldn't have arrived sooner," Mrs. Spratt said and cast a suspicious glance at my table as if I or one of my companions was at fault for the delay created by the storm.

I shrugged, Miss Devin waved an incense stick, and Mrs. Twitcher clutched Sir Lancelot to her chest.

"Really, the sort of people who are allowed on board these days," Mrs. Spratt muttered. "What say you, Mr. Spratt?"

The man shrugged and focused on eating.

"Shall we?" I suggested to my companions as other passengers hurried outside to catch their first glimpse of the Suez Canal.

"Oh, no," Mrs. Twitcher said. "I won't be risking my precious parrot again."

"You mean my parrot, you foul murderer," Mr. Twitcher shouted from his perch on the table near us.

His wife was oblivious to Mr. Twitcher's insults,

but Miss Devin turned and hushed him. Her behavior only confirmed Mrs. Spratt's dim opinion of my companions, for she stood up and grasped her husband by the arm.

"I believe we need some fresh air, Mr. Spratt," she declared. "Air that isn't contaminated with insanity."

I left Mr. and Mrs. Twitcher to their squabbling, one-sided though it may be. I suspected Mr. Twitcher would regain his energy and continue to haunt his wife. But with the parrots hiding somewhere in the ship, they only had Sir Lancelot to fight over, and I didn't blame the other birds for wanting no part in it.

"Miss Knight, a word," Chief Engineer Rocky said as I started to follow the other passengers to the front of the ship.

"Of course. And thank you for all your assistance."

He nodded, his eyes cutting furtively from side to side. "You have it, don't you?"

I did my best to hide my surprise. "Do I have what, sir?"

"The pyramid."

"You knew of it?"

He nodded. "A mutual friend who is waiting for

us at the port requested that I keep an eye out for your safety."

"And that's why you were so liberal with Pip's time."

He nodded.

"Never fear, sir. We shall complete our mission."

The moment was anti-climactic. Chief Officer Frenchy didn't have a choice in keeping Prof. Runal in the brig once we'd dropped anchor at the port of Cairo. When the chief engineer mentioned the matter to the captain, the captain immediately ordered a chastised Frenchy to release the good professor at once as there was no harm done that couldn't be repaired before the return trip.

By the time Prof. Runal joined me on the upper deck, three men in military uniform had boarded the ship and were on deck, chatting with the chief engineer. He gestured toward us, and the officer with the most medals and badges on his jacket approached us, his stride sharp and precise. He bowed at Prof. Runal and ignored my presence.

"I trust your trip was a pleasant and uneventful one?" His voice was smooth and reminded me of used cooking oil.

"Indeed, sir. It was quite so. Not a fuss or bother."

"And you have the artifact about which I wrote to you?"

"I do. My associate and I have kept it quite close at hand. Very close, indeed."

The officer still didn't bother to look at me, and I felt a deep urge to introduce him to the top of my walking stick. I held both my tongue and the stick close to me.

"The Empire is indebted to you. Now, if you please."

Prof. Runal turned and nodded at me. Only then did the officer glance my way, a mixture of surprise marring his cool expression.

Without a word, I retrieved the pyramid from my purse and handed it to the professor, who bounced it on his palm before giving it to the officer.

An expression crossed the officer's features, and I squinted at his energy for a brief moment. What I saw confirmed Alexander's story. There was a flicker of violence and a sense of undeserved victory before the man resumed his emotionless exterior.

"My nation thanks you," he said and tipped his head at Prof. Runal, then twirled on a heel and marched back to his two companions.

"Quite singular. Quite unusual indeed," Prof. Runal said.

"What's that, sir?"

The three officers descended the gangplank and disappeared into the hectic crowds of the port.

The professor bounced on his heels. "I could've sworn the pyramid was a tad lighter than I remember it, as if something was missing."

"Really, sir?"

"Yes, really. Truly. A most peculiar situation. I can't imagine how that's possible."

"Neither can I, sir."

"Shall we go for tea? I hear the cook's made that chocolate pudding you enjoy."

I smiled and met his knowing glance. "I believe a cup of tea is very much in order. I'll join you in the dining room shortly."

I waited until he retreated inside before strolling toward the other side of the ship, away from the dock. I leaned against the railing and stared out at the ocean. Something rubbed against my legs. I glanced down at the black cat.

"It seems you bring good luck, after all," I said.

The cat meowed and sat next to me, her tail twitching around her legs.

"I'll have you know parrots are an exceptional species," Mr. Twitcher shouted. "Their intelligence easily surpasses many humans I've met, including — I dare say — you, Mr. Knight."

"Have you never heard the expression *bird brain*, Mr. Twitcher?" Gideon asked.

The two ghosts were a few feet away from me. I glanced toward them just as Gideon made a rude gesture, then pirouetted out of Mr. Twitcher's enraged reach. While I didn't want to encourage Gideon's mischievousness, I smiled. How I had missed him. And now ... Now I could have him back in my life, even if in a limited form. Unless I took my medicine.

I reached into my pocket and retrieved the tin box. It rattled with satisfying fullness. Inside lay the key to my retirement, for I would be rather useless to the Society if I was numb. Numb and normal, with decades of human normalcy stretching out before me.

A normal life awaited me, thanks to the contents of the box. Maybe there was even the possibility of a bit of happiness among people who weren't trying to kill me.

"Beatrice, darling, shall we hide the stuffed parrot?" Gideon asked.

"You scalawag!" Mr. Twitcher yelled, and the two floated through the deck to a lower level.

"A normal life would definitely be quieter," I told the cat. "But think of all I'd miss."

I opened the tin box and stared at the pills. They looked like bits of chalk, yet they contained the power to render me as limited in second sight as my fellow passengers. I held the box over the water and tilted it.

Little pills of normalcy rained down into the waves. When the box was quite empty, I clicked the lid closed with a satisfying *snap*, like the sound the last piece of a puzzle makes when the mystery is finally solved.

The cat purred, and I picked her up. "Don't worry, Cairo. It's a great decision. And if I'm being honest, normalcy is terribly overrated."

The End...

Beatrice Knight has survived another misadventure with African paranormal and supernatural beings, but more await. Join Miss Knight as she embarks on her greatest — and possibly most perilous — adventure yet when she moves to the colonial town of Nairobi, Kenya. She'll need more than tea and good manners if she's to unravel the mysteries awaiting her in the Society for Paranormals Cozy Mystery series.

Fact & Fiction

Allow me to clarify what parts of this story are based on some semblance of reality. Below are the facts as I understand them, and the fictional aspects pointed out.

During breakfast, Mr. Steward entertained his family and horrified his wife with a recitation of the news, almost all of which was factual.

Fact: In 1898 (the year this story occurs), the Spanish-American war was officially declared.

Fact: Mr. Steward also informed a much-aggrieved Mrs. Steward that the Bubonic Plague was alive and well, particularly in China and India. The third bubonic plague pandemic began in 1855 and spread around the world, killing more than 12 million in India and China.

Fact: The Mahdist War was between the Mahdist Sudanese (led by religious leader Muhammad Ahmad bin Abd Allah) and the Egyptian forces who were later joined by the British forces.

Fiction: A small pyramid didn't contain the key (literal or metaphorical) to ending that or any other war.

Fiction: A pair of museum thieves weren't ravaging British institutions and robbing them of antiquities that the colonial power had stolen from others.

Fact: The first driver to die from injuries sustained in a motoring accident was (as Mr. Steward explained) Mr. Henry Lindfield of Brighton when his electrical carriage overturned on 12 February 1898. This was well before the regular use of seatbelts and airbags.

Fiction: There was no steamship called the S.S. *Suez* as far as I know. Then again, I hardly know everything.

Fact: However, Google is better informed than I am. And according to the combined power of Google and Wikipedia, a Japanese passenger-cargo ship called S.S. *Suez Maru* did exist.

Fact: Steamships were surprisingly fast when compared to modern freight ships, and it's more than likely that a steamship could make the journey from London to Cairo in well under two weeks. Having the Suez Canal (opened in 1869) certainly sped up the trip.

Fact: In 1898, Will Kellogg invented Corn Flakes. This is in no way relevant to Miss Knight or her story, but it's fun to know. And breakfast is an important meal, just as tea is an essential beverage without which there is only misery and chaos.

Fact / Fiction: Vered doesn't live in a mud hut; she prefers a treehouse. Her kids don't ride a zebra to school, as their father uses it to go to work. And monkeys make terrible pets.

Fact: Miss Knight's adventures continue in *Miss Knight & the Ghosts of Tsavo*.

Fact: Vered has other books you need to read, including **ten** Miss Knight adventures in the *Society for Paranormals* series. You'll also enjoy the *Wavily Witches* series which is set in modern-day Kenya.

Fact: Pick up the *Society* prequel for free. *Miss Knight & the Night in Lagos* tells the adventure of Miss Knight's first visit to Africa where she meets Koki the Mantis. Visit https://sterlingandstone.net/

night-in-lagos/ to get your copy as well as other gifts.

Fact: Normalcy is terribly overrated.

What to read next

Want more of the magic of Vered Ehsani's cozy mysteries in your life and on your Kindle? Then you are in luck! Download Storm Wavily and the Pirate King to start the Pirates Ahoy Cozy Mystery Series next!! Available to read for free with your Kindle Unlimited Membership.

Get Miss Knight and the Ghosts of Tsavo Today!

A Note from the Author

Thank you for reading *Miss Knight and the Pyramid's Puzzle.*

If you enjoyed this book, please consider writing a review of it on your favorite bookselling site so other readers can enjoy it too. Just a couple of sentences would mean a lot to me.

Thank you!

Vered Ehsani

About the Author

Vered Ehsani has been a writer since she could hold pen to paper, which is a *lot* longer than she cares to admit. Her work in engineering, environmental management and with the United Nations has taken her around the world. She lives in Kenya with her family and various other animals.

The monkeys in her backyard inspire Vered to create fun, upbeat adventures with a supernatural twist. She enjoys playing with quirky, witty characters who don't quite fit the template for 'normal' despite their best efforts. She's perfectly comfortable exploring the brighter side of human nature.

Are you looking for a mind-refreshing dip into a charming, fanciful world? Then welcome. Sit down with a cup of tea and prepare to be reminded that life can be a delightful place.

Write to vered (vered@sterlingandstone.net) — she loves connecting with her readers!

Also By Vered Ehsani

Society for Paranormals

Miss Knight and the Night in Lagos

Miss Knight and the Ghosts of Tsavo

Miss Knight and the Automaton's Wife

Miss Knight and the Mantis' Revenge

Miss Knight and the Fourth Mandate

Miss Knight and the Nandi's Curse

Miss Knight and the Spider's Web

Miss Knight and the Stones of Nairobi

Miss Knight and the Wedding Killer

Miss Knight and the Throne of Death

Miss Knight and the Poacher's Catch

Miss Knight and the Pyramid's Puzzle

Wavily Witches

Witch Way To Go

Witch Time For Tea

Witch Bat To Swing

Witch Law To Break

Witch Demon to Trust

Witch Bride To Chase

Witch Ghost To Hunt

The Pirates Ahoy Cozy Mysteries

Storm Wavily and the Pirate King

Storm Wavily and the Sea Lord

Storm Wavily and the Lost Treasure

Storm Wavily and the Ghost Town

Storm Wavily and the Secret Society

The Next Evolution

Transition

Convergence

Evolution

Stand Alone Novels

The Christmas Camel

The Last Ten Minutes

the hAPPening